AN EMBASSY AFFAIR

MANUEL CABELLO GALVÁN

The original of this book has been recorded in the Territorial Register of the Intellectual Property of Andalucia and tralated into English by the author.

Date: November 2016
File number: 1045-16
Reg. number: 2016999003436465

This novel is a work of fiction. Names, places or details incidents are the product of the author´s imagination or used as fiction.

Any resemblance to real events, situations or characters, alive or dead, is pure coincidence.

INDICE:

THE CALL

Theodore waited for Claudia on the lintel at the front door of the apartment, while she picked up the handbag from the dresser. They were going for a walk in the park. The day had been hot, and the afternoon was beginning to cool down, which inviting to go out for a walk.

Later, they would return along the Grand Boulevard, after having dinner at the restaurant-cafeteria, The Golden Eagle.

They were about to leave, when is heard the sound of a phone in Theodore's office. Claudia shows a displeased gesture in her face. If she would not had taken so long to get from the dressing room her bag, they whould be out now, and he would not have to answer the call.

The phone continues ringing insistently. Theodore does not like having to attend the phone call proceeded from the private phone in his office. He picked it up, and on the other side of the phone, he heard a familiar voice, accompanied by the expression. At last!

- Yes Paul! What is the reason for your call? I fear your calls on this phone. You never give me good news.

- That is what friends are for. We miss you so much. -- There was a pause. -- Theo, sorry to bother you, but I need your help. Although it's really the Agency that needs you. It is a very important and delicate matter. The order comes from the highest instance, which has assigned to the agency. It is highly confidential.

- What's happening, Paul? Don't you have enough staff that you have to call me? You know I've been off duty for a long time.

- Sorry, Theo, I can't tell you anything else on the phone. The orders coming from above, to the big boss. They have asked him for the best, and he has suggested me, that I require your services. Sorry, but you have to come. He will personally inform you about the matter. Once you are up to date, whether you accept or not, it will be your own decision. Believe me! Your decisión will be respected. You have a flight and ticket reserved, for tomorrow at eleven hours, in the Pan Am Company. I will be waiting for your arrival at the airport, and from there, we will go directly to see the big boss.

- All right, Paul. I will be there. See you tomorrow. Goodbye.

Claudia remained in the hall of the apartment. She had inadvertently overheard the entire conversation. Her heart skipped a beat inside her. From what she had heard, she would be deprived of her husband's company, not knowing how long. He would be away for the misión untrusted. Theodore would have to go on a trip.

Lately, she always accompanied him on his trips, but this was not a pleasure trip, it was a very special trip. She knew that her husband could not reject it, which would force her to remain at home alone during his absence, with the uncertainty of his return.

- Was that call official or am I wrong? -- She asks with a slight and nervous voice. – Please, can you tell me what is it about?

- I really don't know what this is about. You know that by phone, they don´t give any information. I think must be a very important matter. Paul said me the call came directly from the big boss. Now, I am obliged to go. I cannot refuse it and you know it. I will leave first time tomorrow. You know well how much I regret leaving you here.

Claudia, with a smile, tried to appear normal, but since she knew her husband's true profession, they could call him at any time. They considered him one of the best, perhaps the best, and she had no choice, to accept it with all its consequences.

Theodore approached with a smile and taking her by the waist, he pulled her gently, kissing her lovingly. Then he closed the door and they went out into the street.

They walked along the Grand Boulevard in silence, until they reached the cafeteria-restaurant The Golden Eagle. Once there, they had settled into their seats. Claudia could not hold it any longer and broke the silence.

- Well, dear. Please! Is there anything else I should know? You haven't spoken a single word since we left home. I have the impression that I will pass a long while alone at home, without your company.

- Paul, just told me, it is a very delicate and important matter. Believe me! I don´t know anything about it, nor did where they will send me and how long I will be away.

They remained in the cafeteria until nightfall. They returned home, holding their arm. They walked slowly and silently, as if they wanted to stop time. During the walking back home, neither of them wanted to break it.

However, they din´t like the idea of separating.

-oo0oo-

11

TRIP TO WASHINGTON, D.C.

Upon landing the flight of Pan Am, at Washington-Dulles Airport, Theodore carried only one sportbag. He was one of the first passengers to leave the airport compound. He didn't have to wait to collect luggage. Without more, he headed straight for the exit, where his boss and friend, Paul Blanchard was waiting for him.

They greeted each other with a handshake and followed by a hug. Without wasting time, they head to the airport car park. They get into the car whose driver awaited them.

During the drive to the headquarters, only silence had inside the vehicle. Discretion, among others, was one of Theodore's great qualities. He was highly regarded for his career, as one of the best agents of the agency, since its foundation.

With his work, he had created an infallible agent status within the agency. He had always managed to solve all the entrusted cases cleanly, without leaving any clues. Very few were the people who knew him as a special secret agent.

They arrived at a huge and modern building, located in the center of the city. The vehicle is heading to the rear of the building. Using a remote control, the garage door opened. As soon as they enter, the door closes automatically. Descend to the second floor. Where the car parked.

They went to one of the elevators in the parking, which took them to the seventh floor. Paul used his magnetic card and automatically opened the door with access to the office. As soon as its opened, they went inside, facing a security guard.

After going through the security control. They enter a huge hallway. At the end the office number 720 was. A sign on the

outside of the door of the office indicated, A.S. Import &
Export International.

Paul Blanchard used his magnetic card to open again the
office Agency door. As soon as they entered met the big
boss´s secretary. She was a woman, about forty years, slender
and thin. Her bearing was stately and very attractive. She wore
the lasted model of Tous brand optical glasses.

- Hello Paul, I am glad to see you -- Miss Margaret greets him.
-- How long without seeing you. What brings you here?

- Hello Margaret. You know well what brings me here!

- The big boss! -- Margaret answers, with a wry smile on her
lips. -- Come on. He is waiting for you.

Paul knocked with the knuckles of his right hand the door of
the chief and they enter in the office. It was a huge office. On
the right-hand side, the big boss, Nicholas Smith was sitting in
a large fluffy leather chair behind a fancy mahogany table.

In front of the table were two leather-trimmed armchairs as the
same color of the table.

- Hello chief, this is our agent, Theodore W. Georges.

Nicholas Smith appeared to be the same age as Theodore. For
the position in the Agency organization, he considered himself
a relatively young. Emanated confidence and personality,
accompanied by soft and exquisite manners.

Theodore not fooled by his outward appearance. He knows
positively that behind his kindness, hided a strong character.
Any suggestion was an order. He didn´t have to raise his voice
to be obeyed, without questioning.

He greeted Theodore, shaking hands effusive and warmly.

- Hello Theodore, I have long wanted to meet you personally. Although, to tell the truth, from the records of your performed services which have in our departments, I have the impression that I have always known you. I know you´re married, and practically, you're off active duty. However, we have a serious problem in one of our embassies in the Eastern countries. Lately, there is a leak of secret documents detected, affecting both our national security and our embassy in that country.

- Let me make an observation. I suppose our embassy police will be working on this matter. -- Theodore replies. – I suppose that not all embassy staff will have direct access to such documents and classified files.

- Effectively. We believe that not all embassy staff are involved. We believe that only three or four of our staff are authorized to handle such documents. But despite the vigilance they are subjected to, we have not evidences of who the person may be, who subtracts the documents.

The meeting lasted almost four hours. One by one, all the files of the staff working at the embassy were studied, beginning with the ambassador. Even the files of the american security police, which was in charge of custody the embassy, were checked.

They concluded without mistake of being wrong, that the only three persons had access to document manipulations, were; the ambassador, his secretary and the commercial delegate. Logically, for them the investigation would begin. That would be the starting point.

However, sometimes what it seems to be, is not and the contrary. So that, he only possibility to clear this matter up, is to go there to investigate.

Any information on secret or confidential documents, at this time of the cold war, was paid generously.

- This is all, Theo. We will introduce you as one employee. Logically you are going to fill a retirement vacancy for one of our employees.

- I agree. When should I rejoin my new destination?

- As soon as possible. We are aware that documents continue to being pulled with impunity. We have to cut that leaking immediately. Although, they do not know that the documents that we are sending them lately are falses. However, we have to keep sending to make them believe that we know nothing about this matter. If possible, I would like you to present yourself at the embassy as a new employee by next Monday. You will work alone and without help. If you need help, if you really need it, you can count on the embassy's security police chief, Kenneth Díaz. But by the moment, you have to work alone, you can't trust anyone.

- Okay. I will manage this situation alone. I will do with the utmost discretion possible. I prefer to be assigned, initially, for the night service in the surveillance control room, to be able to work time to check the recordings of the surveillance tapes recorded lately inside the embassy.

- Don't worry, when the time comes to make yourself known, you can have everything you need in your investigation. If necessary, you will have more authority than the ambassador himself. It's a saying!

After the meeting, Paul Blanchard and Theodore left the building. The same car drove them back to the airport. Paul said goodbye to his friend Theo, wishing him goodluck in the mission entrusted.

-oo0oo-

DESTINATION MINSK, BELARUS

Before taking the flight to Minsk, Theodore stops by the Dallas-Dulles International Airport bookshop, located in the duty free shop area. He bought a Belarus tourist guide, the country where was sent. Although separated from Russia, they still maintained part of their trade alliance.

On this mission, as always, Theodore decides to travel under the pseudonym of Jack Brown. Whenever is sent on a mission, takes care not to use his real name, so as not to leave any clues to his true address. Actually, many agents do it.

Never before, they never sent him to a mission to that country. He knew that, although it did not belong to the USSR, it was ruled by an iron dictatorship, who maintained order and stability throughout the country.

The airport's megaphone system returns to reality, requesting the attention of passengers, for boarding with the Pan Am Co. flyght to London, where he would transfer for the next flight to Minsk.

He puts the book in his travel bag along with the few items of clothing he carried. From experience, he usually travelled light of luggage. It would not be the first nor the last time that he had to leave a country, without luggage and without its exit customs stamp on his passport.

After the police control, he got on the bus, which will transport the passengers from the airport terminal to boarding area.

Once inside the plane, the flight attendant acommodated him in a first class seat, for the flight to London Heathrow Airport.

Upon arrival, he will have to transfer to the Lot Air Co. Flight destination Minsk, capital of Belarus.

He slided into his seat, and took out of his bag the book; he had bought as a tourist guide about Belarus. He opens the book and begins his reading to know the way of live and habit of that small country. According to the UN nomenclature, it was officially the Republic of Balarus or Belarus. Formerly, called White Russian.

Currently, it is a sovereign landlocked country within Eastern Europe that, until June 1991, it was part of the Union of Soviet Socialist Republics.

It was located in the center and surrounded by other countries, which had also belonged to the USSR.

Its extension is 207,600 km2. Its limits are clearly defined; to the north with Lithuania and Latvia, to the east with the Russian Federation, to the south with Ukraine and to the west with Poland.

Its population is about nine and a half million inhabitants. Within the same state, divided into six provinces:

In Minskaya, there is the capital of the country, Minsk. Located in the center of the country. In addition, it has other important cities, such as; Barisv, Molodechno, Salihorsk and Slutsk.

Vitebsk. - Important cities, which are recommended to visit; Vitebsk, Lyepyel, Orsha, Pastavy and Polotsk.

Mahilyowska. - Recommended cities; Maguilov, Asipovichy, Babruisk and Krychov.

Homyelskaya. - Recommended cities; Gomel, Zhytkavichy, Mozir, Rechytsa, and Zhlobin.

Brestskaya. - Recommended cities; Baranovichi, Brest, Byaroza, Kobryn, Luninyets and Pinsk.

Grodno. - Recommended Cities; Grodno, Lida and Vaükaviysk.

He immersed in reading of this interesting and unknown country, when the flight attendant gently called his attention, to serve him dinner. He had been so absorbed in the reading that he had not paid attention to the megaphony system that moments before had informed the passengers that dinner would scrvcd.

- Sir, ¿do you want I serve your dinner? Tell me the drink you are going to have!

- Yes please. Excuse me. Serve me with dinner a beer and a bottle of mineral water.

The flight attendant places the folding table in a horizontal position, and place the tray with the dinner, the beer and the bottle of mineral water.

After dinner serviced, through the megaphony system informs passengers that the three-hour movie Cabaret, starring Liza Minelli will be broadcast during the flight.

Jack Brown preferred to skip the film. He'd seen it on more tan one occasion. To reading of the book about Belarus, it attracted him more.

He was much more interested in knowing details about the country he usually was sent to. For him all the missions were important and in one way or another, he liked to be aware, and especially to know the cities to which was destined.

Minsk, the country's capital, was the Administrative Place of the Commonwealth of Independent States. Two rivers, the Nyamiha and the Svisloch, crossed it.

In addition, has the Belarusian State University of Economics. As well as, with a fascinating, story. According to its reading, the capital was destroyed during the Second World War.

The book served as a tourist guide, too. It recommended visiting the capital and its main monuments, such as; the Cathedral of the Holy Spirit, where the icon of the Mother of God, the most valued in the Sacred Enclosure, displayed inside.

In addition, it recommend visiting for being also of great tourist interest, Mirsky Castle, founded by Prince Ilyinich.

Despite being ardently interested in reading a book, in order to know better such an interesting country, without realizing the fatigue overcoming him and without realizing he plunges into a deep sleep. The book slipped out of his hands and fell to the airplane floor.

-ooOoo-

<u>ARRIVAL TO MINSK, BELARUS</u>

It was Mondey, ten in the morning. The flight attendant thru megaphony asked passengers to fasten their seat belts. The flight of the Cía. Lot Air was about to take land at Minsk International Airport.

Jack Brown stretched out in his seat, was numb from so many hours of sitting flight. He traveled without disguise and dressed normally. His passport indicated an employee adjunct to the business office of the American embassy. He only wore sunglasses and a wide false mustache.

He passed the police and customs control, without difficulty, he was carrying light luggage. A handbag.

At the airport exit, a taxi was waiting for him to transfer him to the embassy. But before going to the embassy, he asked the driver to take him to the Markesal Hotel, where he had a room reserved.

The Markesal Hotel is a standard category, suitable for hard-working people, without great emoluments. Centrally located, next to the shopping streets, next to the main avenue, and a half hour walk from the embassy. He would stay there from then on.

At the hotel reception, he presented his passport. He reserved the room previously by internet. The room number, was two hundred and twelve on the second floor, which faced the back of the hotel, overlooking a small pedestrian street.

His passport was required to register at the hotel. He went up to his room and left his travel bag. Then, he moved to the embassy.

He dropped off the taxi at the main door of the embassy building.

A surveillance camera controlled access from outside.

Two american police watched the consulate front door. As he approaches the entrance, one of them with sergeant gallons, was on duty at the reception control, approaches, greeting him martially.

- Good morning sir. May I help you?

- Yes, I have been assigned to this embassy. My instructions are to introduce myself to Mr. Mark Schneider, immediately. -- He delivers the destination letter to him. -- They are waiting for my immediate incorporation.

The policeman on duty was a serious and circumspect. He reads carefully the document, which communicates the destination of Jack Brown to the embassy, with an immediate order to present himself to the chief of staff, Mr. Mark Schneider.

The officer returns the letter to Jack, and instructs his partner to accompany him to the office. He waited a few minutes to introduce to Mr. Schneider.

- Mr. Brown. -- A voice is heard coming from the end of the office. – Please, come in.

As soon as he enters, the door closed behind him. The chief of the embassy staff, Mr. Schneider stood from his seat to greet the new employee. While, Jack approached to greet him, too, they examine each other with their gaze.

Chief of Staff Mark Schneider was a serious man. Greets and welcomes him cordially.

Mr. Schneider likes the new employee appointed to. During the five minutes that the interview lasted, he considered him as an educated person, perfectly prepared and easy going, with an enormous desire to work.

- At first, you will occupy the place of a person who has retired. You will occupy his stall in the security control. You will take in charge for the night service in the watchroom of the embassy. I hope you enjoy your job.

- If that is all, Mr. Schneider, with your permission I will go to the hotel, I need to rest, since yesterday I have not closed an eye. The change of schedule makes me feel a little tired, so for the moment I will rest during the day and work at night. This will not affect me to work at night, the change of time benefits me, also. I do not think there is any impediment on the part of other colleagues.

- Sure not. Don´t worry.

When he left the embassy and took a taxi to the Markesal Hotel. He was tired. The night before the trip, Claudia had barely let him sleep, fearing for his safety and harassing him with questions. She was nervous and afraid of what it might happen to him in an unknown and dangerous country.

Like the night before, he had barely rested the first three hours on board the plane of the Lot Co. The flight had not been too smooth. It had many turbulence difficulties. The plane was old, medium-sized and with many hours of flight. It should be out of service.

In one of the aerial potholes due to turbulence, many of the luggage placed in the shelves above the passenger seats opened, falling on the passengers and on the plane floor.

He was looking forward to the hotel to rest.

-oo0oo-

As soon as he went up, closed the door of the room and ran the window curtains darkening the room. Then meticulously checked if there was any micro video camara or listening device.

Apparently, everything was in order in the room. He couldn´t find nothing strange. Until he carefully picked up the phone in the room, checking that was a listening microphone installed inside. It wasn´t of the most modern and sophisticated one, but still provided good service. It didn't surprise him.

When he went to hang down, he heard the receptionist's voice asking him if he was happy with the room, or if he wanted something. This confirmed his thoughts. He knew he was under close surveillance.

- No thanks. I was just checking to see if I could make calls abroad from this phone, in case I needed to call my ex-wife, to ask her about my children.

- Sir, let me inform you. If you want to make a call within the country, dial number nine, if it is outside the country, all calls will be through the operator of the hotel switchboard.

- Thank you so much. I'll take a bath and go to bed. Please, I wish not to be disturbed.

As usual, he locked and bolted the door to the room with the desk chair. He checked the window facing the avenue. It was difficult to access.

Then, he got into bed. He fell asleep immediately.

-oo0oo-

HE BEGINS TO WORK

The alarm went off on his wristwatch. The sound startled him, he didn´t expect it. It was seven thirty in the afternoon. He remained in bed for another fifteen minutes. The time he took to clarify and put his ideas in order.

He dined at the hotel restaurant. He ordered a beefsteak with fries potatos and a jug of beer. For dessert, apple pie and a cup of strong black coffee.

On leaving the restaurant, on the sidewalk in front of the hotel, there was a bus stop. Next to the canopy of the bus stop, a map of the city with information on the main monuments, metro and bus line timetables.

He crossed the avenue and consulted the timetable and the map of the city bus lines. He took line number five. It would drop him off at the Narensdka Square bus stop, which was about a five-minute walk from the embassy.

He arrived at the embassy twenty minutes before the time he had to take his job. Like all employees, he entered through the back door of the building. The control service door for staff.

When he reached to its height, the surveillance camera was tracking his movements. Jack Brown took out his ID card by running it through the scanner. Automatically, the door opened, ushering in the new employee.

The door closed as soon as he was inside. There was a small entrance, that led to an anteroom, which had an armored glass door, from which could be seen to the other side a couple of military police, who carried out the surveillance control of the door and the building surroundings.

Jack Brown was accustomed to this kind of security used in official buildings. Everything was normal. He ran his ID card through the second scanner again. The door opened automatically. He went to the table where the two police officers were sitting.

He showed his identity card, to the police officer who was sat down by the window. The police officer was surprised by the presence of this employee. They had not reported from the personnel department to the security department about this employee. He checked the list of the staff of the embassy through his computer, checking that appears on the monitor, along with his current photo.

The companion checked his handbag carefully. There was nothing special inside. Maybe one sandwich and a utility knife. The policeofficer kindly escorted him to his workplace.

His job was monitoring through the watchroom, the interior of the embassy. The watchroom was equipped with sophisticated surveillance equipment.

In the watchroom surveillance, was Frank Pierson. He was a brilliant young man of forty and a computer engineer. He brought him up to date on how to use of monitors and the surveillance cameras.

The room had a small dressing room with several lockers for the personal use of the employees. The lockers were closed, except one that was open. The key was in the locker. He took the key tucking his bag inside. He closed it, keeping the key in his pocket.

The night passed quietly concerning the vigilance. Frank spent the night talking him. He boasted of being a great expert in the matter.

Jack listened to everything that Frank Pierson said about the embassy or commented. He bragged about knowing his job perfectly. For him the technology had no secret. He could modify and fix the recording content of any tape, without noticing the fix.

-ooOoo-

A few days later, another colleague, Patrick Riarson, who took the place of Frank Pierson. This had a different personality than Frank. He was more introverted, despite being a little younger. He had a little difficulty. He was limping on his right leg.

One night, when they were both on surveillance, Jack realized that something happened to his new companion. Patrick's face denoted pain. He thought it was time to hold a conversation. They had barely spoken to each other. He appeared to be a good person, but closed in himself.

- Sorry, Patrick. Is something wrong with you? I notice that you aren´t feeling well. I see that you have a bad face, as if you were sick.

 - Don't worry, Jack. It's about my right leg. I have a terrible pain that is killing me. I have been running out of pills for several days. Currently, I cannot pass without them.

- Good. If I can do something to help you, trust on me. I have no problem covering you. If you want, you can go to a pharmacy and buy them. I'll take charge of the surveillance during your absence.

- Thanks Jack. But, remember is totally forbidden to abandon surveillance. Must be a very special reason. Anyway, they sent me the pills by diplomatic pouch from our country. I cannot buy the pills here. The problem is that lately the pills arrive with more delay than normal.

 - I suppose there will be a very special reason that causes this delay. -- He comments, apparently, not interest. He wanted to know, if the staff of the embassy were awared the problem of the extraction of the documents. -- Is there any problem in the delay?

- I suppose there will be. But I do not know it.

Jack takes advantage of Patrick. He was communicative and talkative, to ask him about the tapes recorded.

- Frank, I'm curious to know if the embassy keeps the recorded tapes. I suppose they will keep in a safe place.

 - Right in the closet behind us. They are all of them archived chronologically by dates. Why do you ask. What do you want to know?

 - Not for nothing. At the last embassy where I worked on, if nothing happened, they reused the tapes again, after erasing previous recordings.

Jack considered inappropriated to continue asking him about the tapes. He changed the conversation not to raise suspicions. He already knew what interested him.

- Do you mind if I ask you a personal question? -- Patrick nodded. -- What is the ailment that causes the pain?

 - Of course not. I did the military service in the navy, as a marine. I reached the rank of lieutenant. I stationed for two years in Vietnam. During one of the many clashes with the Vietcong, a piece of shrapnel hit my right knee, destroying it. At first, I thought I would lose my leg, but after many surgery operations, I thanks to God and Dr. Newman saved my leg, but in return, I have to carry the aftermath, which cause me horrible pain. In compensation for the services rendered, when I licensed, they offered me an employ in the government. I accepted it. It was the best thing that happened to me, and I had no other choice, many other colleagues of mine, have not had my luck. Some are unemployed, wandering the streets of the cities, and living poorly. Thanks, God I can say that I have been very lucky.

- I'm sorry. Sometimes life is not as we think. Anyway, I keep my offer. If you need to have a rest, you can do it, I'll take care of the surveillance. Do not worry about me, take advantage now, the night is quite.

- If you don't mind, I'll rest for a few minutes. If something happens, please call me.

Inside the surveillance watchroom, there was a smaller room, which used as a dressing room. It had a bench with the seat upholstered. The one used to rest sometimes.

Shortly after lying down, Patrick fell asleep.

Jack Brown settled into his seat. He kept thinking about the conversation with Patrick.

He took advantage of the fact that Patrick had fallen asleep to rummage through the wardrobe´s drawers in the surveillance room. He found nothing that could incriminate those who worked there.

He tried to open the closet where the video tapes were kept, but could not get his purpose. The door was locked. He searched for it, but could not find it. However, he did not try to force the lock to avoid raising suspicions, and also, his partner Patrick, could catch him red-handed.

Two hours before dawn. Patrick was still sleeping. Perhaps, he would have relaxed and relieved of the pain of having his leg resting. It was time to wake him up.

- Patrick, wake up. -- He called him and touching him lightly on the shoulder.

- Sorry Jack. I'm sorry! I couldn't help falling asleep. I had been at home for several days without being able to sleep. Have there been any news?

- Calm down! Nothing happened. Everything went well; otherwise, I would have called you. Also, I already told you, remember that you could trust on me. We're companions. No?

- Thanks, Jack. But if we are caught outside our surveillance post, we will be sanctioned and now, I cannot afford it.

- Tell it to me. My ex-wife takes half of my pay. To live comfortably with her boyfriend, whom I am supporting. The bastard doesn't work. It is what it is. And you Patrick are you married?

- No. I'm a bachelor. I was about to get married. My girlfriend Erika, on my return licensed from Vietnam, I found that she married a friend of mine, who took my place consoling her, during the time I was in Vietnam. Later, through some friends, I knew that he had not been the only one; she had been with, during my absence. I don't hold a grudge against her. By the contrary, she has done me a great favor. From what I know of her, she is having a hard time, too. Unfortunately, she is divorced and there is a child involved.

- I'm sorry. But, what you tell me, I'm glad that didn't happen to you. I hope you find the woman of your life. The one you deserve it. You are a good person.

That morning, when Jack left the embassy, he was greatly disappointed. He had not advanced in the investigation.

In addition, with his companion Patrick during surveillance hours, he could not move freely. He felt handcuffed.

-ooOoo-

He took bus number eight; take him back to the Markesal Hotel. Along the way, he made a plan. He would start it that night.

Before going up to his room, he went into the hotel restaurant and ate an opulent breakfast. He had not had a bite since dinner the night before, and was hungry.

During breakfast, he realized that in the restaurant tap, there was an individual, who had gotten on the bus at the same stop.

When finished breakfast he went up his bedroom.

-ooOoo-

That night, when he arrived at the embassy, he used the same procedure as the night before. Passed two doors through the scanner, plus the police control.

The police officers knew him. They greet him, without patting him down. Sometimes the multiuse knife, made the scanner ring, put it in one of the trays used for that purpose and passed the knife.

When he got to the security control watchroom, his partner Patrick had not yet arrived. He was not worried; on the contrary, he could work freely without his presence. Surely it would be about to arrive.

Patrick didn't take long to arrive. He was exasperated, the pain was killing him and the eye dark circles reached his cheeks.

- Sorry Jack. Sorry for the delay. I have had a terrible day. I could not sleep a wink all the day. I have passed by the office of Mr. Sieman, the person in charge of receiving the mail, and he informs me that the diplomatic valise in which my pills come has not yet arrived. I need them the calm these horribles pains.

- I think I can help you. Although I haven't told you anything. I was in Korea and I have a piece of shrapnel on my shoulder, sometimes I need help. I always carry a box of capsules in my travel bag, in case to need them. I hope you don't comment it, nobody knows. They had a good dose of melatonin, if you want; you can take a couple of them. They will relieve your pain and quickly relax you.

- Yes thanks. I'll take them, I can't support the pain anymore It is insufferable, I appreciate it. I hope I don't fall asleep like last night.

- Don't worry. I will cover you.

-ooOoo-

The capsules didn't take long to made effect. He could hardly stand upright sitting in the surveillance chair. There was a moment he almost fell. Jack picked him up and carried him to the dressing room, laying him on the bench. He had not fully laid down when he was asleep.

Jack took the opportunity, to use a kind of picklock from his multiuse knife, to open the closet door, where the recording video tapes were. After several attempts, and at the insistence of the picklock, the lock gave way and the door opened.

He began to review the recorded tapes, which contained the tour of the diplomatic pouch, inside the embassy. From the entrance goes through the police control to the mail reception department, and the people who handled it.

The review began, from four months ago.

In the watchroom, there were two unused screens in perfect conditions. He connected one of them and put it into operation, and worked perfectly. One the cameras aimed at monitoring the private toilets and services used by the staff. He turned it off, leaving it unused, as before it was, because it was forbidden to record inside.

He used the other recorder and the second screen monitor that was also unused, but working perfectly. He put it into operation and began to watch the video tapes.

Occasionally, he could also have a glance at the rest of the monitors. Everything was quiet. A perfect calm reigned. His partner Patrick was in Morpheus arms. He would let him rest until the end of the guard. He would check the duration of the effects of the capsules, for the nights to come.

During the night, he was able to review a month of recording. He checked the tapes with the mail route and the diplomatic pouch inside the embassy. He found nothing. The rest of the tapes, he did not find them interesting.

He was tired. He had watched more than enough tapes for a single night. Patrick, was about to wake up and did not want to be caught "red-handed" in this matter. He would have to give him some explanations, which were not included in the script.

It was almost sunrise. He shook Patrick gently to wake him up. If he wouldn't called, he could have been sleeping for at least a couple more hours.

- Sorry Jack, I slept like a log. Your capsules are magnificent. But, you have taken yourself with surveillance.

- Don't worry I don't care. I did it with pleasure.

He was about to leave, when Miss Donalson informed Jack to report to Mr. Harrelson's office. Jack was surprised and made a strange gesture with his face at the secretary, like a little worried, as if he did not wait for the ambassador's call.

- Miss Donalson, do you know why the ambassador requires me? Am I not doing my job well? Have I committed a fault?

- Sorry, Mr. Brown. I do not know the reason for your call.

He crossed the glass corridor of the embassy's inner courtyard, which led to the ambassador's office. All the staff were at their stalls working.

Miss Blanca Donalson knocks on the door with her knuckles, and from inside heard a voice authorizing them entry.

- Come in, Mr. Brown. The ambassador awaits you. -- Said Miss Donalson.

The door opened. The ambassador was waiting on the end of the office. She motioned for him to pass quickly. Closing the door once inside.

The ambassador was a person in his forties. Tall, blonde-haired person with polite manners. He was elegantly dressed.

- Mr. Brown, nice to meet you. I am sorry, I did not greet you before, I have been busy. I just want to welcome you. ¿Are you comfortable at your work?

Jack Brown had not trusted anyone since he arrived at the embassy, including the ambassador himself. The ambassador was unaware that Jack was a secret agent sent to the embassy, to discover the person or persons involved in the leak of secret documents.

When he entrusted a work, he normally becomes a person of tremendous distrust. He does not know with the difficulties that will encounter, but rather in the danger that it entails. It was not the first time that thanks to his mistrust, and his sixth sense, he had the possibility of continuing to live.

He did not know the reason why the ambassador had called him to his office, but he took advantage of it to inform him that his partner Patrick was ill due to the terrible pain in his right knee.

- Sir, regarding my work I manage perfectly. I feel well and comfortable. The change of schedule benefits me more than worries me. By having the time changed, my life has not altered in the least.

- Great! I'm happy for you. I just wanted to know if you were comfortable with your job. Anything you need, please contact Mr Schneider, our staff chief.

- If you allow me sir, my surveillance partner Patrick Riarson, is not feeling well. As you well know, he has a difficulty in his right knee, due to a war wound. He's waiting for his capsules a week ago, and they still haven't arrived. He has a terrible pain.

- I'll take care of this matter. Thanks for your observation.

He stormed out of the ambassador's office. It lacked of a surveillance video, and it was precisely the place that had to be more protected within the embassy, to prevent an attempt against the ambassador.

He left for the hotel. He would have breakfast in the cafeteria and go to bed.

On the bus back to the hotel, when he got on almost collided with an individual, whom remembered seeing him three times before. Once in the hotel cafeteria and twice on the bus. It was a tall, sallow-colored, cold-eyed individual. It could notice he was carrying a pistol at his belt under his wide jacket.

Jack had no doubt he was a secret agent. He had focused on his work inside the embassy. He had forgotten that watched by the secret pólice of this country.

He sat down at the back of the bus, next to the exit door. The secret police sat in the one of the first seat. From his seat, Jack was able to watch him. He wouldn't forget his sallow face. In fact, his travel bag had searched at the hotel on many times.

-ooOoo-

When he went that evening to the embassy, Mr. Schneider informed him, that Frank Pierson was free of duty, because of his swollen knee. So, he would have to carry out the embassy surveillance without his partner.

Jack put up a face of annoyance, as if to imply that it was too much work for him alone. However, he was happy. Now he would put his plan into action, the one he had been eagerly waiting for.

During the days Patrick was off service, he took advantage to finish reviewing the videotapes carefully. However, he had achieved nothing, put him on the trail of the person, he assumed might be involved in extracting the secret documents.

Lately, he was stuck in the investigation. He could not go forward; he caught in the night shift. From now on, continuing on the night shift would not provide him with more information. Everything had checked and verified.

He would have to see how to get the change for the day shift.

-ooOoo-

But, sometimes things happen when least expecte it. They happens on their own.

Days later, an unforeseein event suddenly arose. Frank Pierson took days of his vacactiones, which he has not previously enjoyed. Patrick should occupy his place. He discharged of service for illness, and then Jack Brown should take his place.

Now, he would take the opportunity, he had been waited so much. To work alone during the day and not raising suspicions. He would check the movement of the embassy staff with complete freedom for the day.

-oo0oo-

MISS BLANCA DONALSON

The surveillance began with Miss Donalson, the ambassador's secretary, to whom would watched, in case she was implicated in the loss of the secret documents.

When he connected the video camera Miss Donalson's was standing, facing a mirror, grooming and molding the paint on her lips.

She always was elegantly dressed. This time, wore a charcoal gray pantsuit, highlighting her white blouse through her jacket and a crocodile skin bag and shoes.

Due to her position as ambassador's secretary, Jack assumed that she could have access and could be duly aware of all the "classified or protected" documents incoming and outgoing the embassy.

On one of the lapels of his jacket, she wore a gold brooch with diamonds, representing the head of a lion.

He spent the whole morning, watching through the monitor her movements. Eny movement was within the most absolute normality. She moved naturally, implying that she was out of the plot.

At the end of the working day, Miss Donalson said goodbye to the ambassador, locking carefuly her desk's drawers, before leaving the office.

-oo0oo-

The weather was rainy. The sky overcast and there was quite a bit of humidity in the air. He took the bus back to the hotel. Not wearing umbrella or raincoat. He didn't want the rain surprised him on halfway to the hotel.

Several days ago, at the bus stop, had coincided with another medium-sized individual, with a grim look and a bad faced. He could seen at a distance of thousand leagues. He was a secret police. He always carried a newspaper under his arm.

At the stop in front of the hotel, he got off the bus and entered the restaurant. He was hungry. He asked for a strong menu for dinner. He had nothing eaten since breakfast and was hungry.

He took small sips from the beer jug, while waiting for dinner. He shifted his gaze to the restaurant counter bar. Sitting on a stool, was the man who followed him, having a coffee. When the latter realized that he was looking at him, he pretended not to play pay attention, unfolding the newspaper, as if to read it.

After dinner, he passed in front the man, without looking at him. He almost touched the newspaper with his arm. As if he didn't exist. Letting him know that he knew he was there and was not afraid of him.

He went up to his room. It was prepared and clean, like every day. Apparently, everything was in perfect order. However, his travel bag had thoroughly searched again. It was not in the position he left it, when went out that morning to work. A zipper of the bag half closed and the closet door badly fitted. The hangers in the closet where his clothes hung did not keep the separation, which he had established.

He locked the door to the room with the desk chair and took a shower before go to bed.

Before getting into bed, he put his watch close to the phone on the nightstand. He noted that he was still "pinched". The watch hands moved wildly. He didn't plan to use it.

Thinking how much missed Claudia lately; it took him longer than usual to fall asleep. It would be, surely due to the tension and accumulated fatigue.

Tomorrow would be another day. He had no other choice.

-oo0oo-

MR. PETER O´CONNOR

The next day, it was the turn to watch over Mr O`Connor, Commercial Delegate of the embassy.

It was a normal-looking individual. Blonde-haired person with incipient baldness. He wore glasses and smiled often. It moved like a cat. His outward appearance was deceptive.

After the ambassador, he was the most important person in the organization chart of the embassy. He had a direct connection to the ambassador's office.

He assumed that by his position, when the ambassador was absent, he would be in charge of acting as ambassador. Very interesting person to take into account.

In addition, he related to executives through the Commertial Delegations of both country. He spoke fluenty the language of the country.

He was an honest man, and an eagerly defender of relations between both countries. However, not for that reason, it could be an obstacle to put aside. He was the most related and well-known person at the embassy. He had been at his job for seven years.

From the monitor connected to the surveillance camera of Mr. O'Connor, Jack observed carefully all the movements was taking place inside the office.

The office of the commercial delegation had two departments. The main office to Mr. O'Connor and other one for two clercks, who were under his charge. His personal secretary, Miss Julie Simpson, and an office officer, Edward Parson was the person in charge of processing outside the embassy, all the official documents relatives to commercial visas, customs clearance, etc.

Edward Parson. An interesting man to consider.

He spent the rest of the morning and part of the afternoon observing both employees. Miss Julie Simpson and Edward Parson.

Although the documents they handled were commercial, and not diplomatic, they were not exempt from surveillance.

He found that they hardly spoke to each other. They just do their jobs.

At the end of his shift, Jack would return to his hotel.

-ooOoo-

MR. SIEMAN

He was the person in charge of receiving the diplomatic pouch. Of Irish descent; tall, dark and strong in his sixties.

Fridays were one of those days when the diplomatic pouch was supposed to arrive. Jack was constantly watching thru the monitor. He did not lose sight of the monitor in this office for a moment. He was waiting for the diplomatic pouch to arrive at any moment.

He would take this opportunity to follow the valise along the way; from the entrance to the embassy until its delivery. It was the most expected moment and perhaps the last step, which would take him to the end of his investigation.

He kept track of Mr. Sieman's department, watching him as did his work, during the morning. At that time, he was in charge of classifying the correspondence to distributing to their respective departments.

He was about to change his monitor when Sergeant Joe McCrea came in carrying the diplomatic pouch. Mr. Sieman took charge of the pouch, after signing the receipt for the delivery of the diplomatic pouch, presented by the sergeant.

Jack, through the monitor follows the route of the diplomatic pouch, until delivered to Miss Donalson. When it reaches this point, it loses sight of the diplomatic pouch. The ambassador's office lacks a surveillance camera. He loses the connection and cannot watch what happens inside.

He assumes that the ambassador would be in charge of opening the diplomatic pouch, in the presence of his secretary. But, having no surveillance camera, he could not see what's going on inside.

Meanwhile, Mr. Sieman waited in Miss Donalson's office to receive instructions concerning to delivery and distribution of the mail to each embassy departments. When Mr. Sieman left Miss Donalson's office, the correspondence carried in his cart didn't indicate anything about, "reserved or confidential."

Jack sees Mr. Sieman come into his office, put the mail on his desk. It classifies it and proceeds to distribute it in the different departments. Observe, through the video camera, how he delivers the mail, and returns to his office.

He had been working a week in the surveillance day control. Everyting had been in vain and unsuccessful. He was getting closer. He was approaching, but could not reach at the end, due to the lack of one surveillance camera in the ambassador's office.

He hoped to have made more progresses during this week. Failing to do so, he decides to take drastic action immediately. He would no longer waste his time. He had no choice but to implement a risky, but it was a final plan.

Sunday was the best day. There was nobody at the embassy, except the military police on duty. He couldn't let it go, otherwise would have to wait another week.

Too long, and time was running out. Tomorrow he would start it up.

He then lef the office.

-oo0oo-

He arrived at the bus stop, just as the bus stopped. He got in and sat in one of the seats in the back that was free. He passed through the corridor, without realizing that he was also traveling sitting on the same bus, one of the secret policemen.

He was so absorbed in his thoughts that until the middle of the journey he did not notice the agent's company. Jack, he was wearing his dark glasses. He appeared to be looking at the streets through which the bus traveled, but in reality, what he was observing was the individual, by the reflection in his glasses.

He reconsidered getting off at the hotel stop. Some users had asked for the next one. He took advantage of the right moment to get off the bus. When the agent noticed the mancuvcr, he didn't have time to react. The bus had started and closed the doors.

Jack watched as the individual quickly rose from his seat, but he had no choice but to continue until the next stop. He knew he wouldn't get rid off him so easily, but would make him work a little harder.

He decided to have dinner in a hamburger-cafeteria, located about ten minutes walking from the hotel. Halfway between the bus stop and the hotel. It was open twenty-four hours.

He was having dinner when the agent showed up. Jack didn't flinch. He didn't give it the slightest importance. He expected to see him from one moment to other. He knew he was one of those bloodhounds, that when he stuck a tooth into a bone he would not leave it until it was finished. He sat down in front of his table. He finished his hamburger and the beer. He got up and ordered a coffee with milk and a piece of cake. He wasnt concerned about the presence of the secret police.

The police also did not try to hide when followed him, it was not necessary. The american was smarter than he imagined. He wasn´t a mere embassy employee. He had no doubt that was a special agent of the american government. But in his files, he had found nothing regarding to this agent. He had even requested information from the secret services and the KGB. They had no information in their files.

Jack did not know the secret police, who was following him. It was Inspector Kustinov, an old dog at work; who sensed that this fifty-year-old american, with an affable and calm appearance was an enemy to reckone with. He didn´t show no sign of fear or concern. His nerves appeared to be of steel. His appearance was as deceptive as it was dangerous. He kept his gaze unblinking as he ate calmly.

After finished his dinner, Jack Brown, walked calmly from the cafeteria directly to the hotel. Knew that Inspector Kustinov was following him. He didn't care; he hadn't committed any crime, so he couldn't stop him. He belonged to the diplomatic service of a foreign embassy. They couldn't stop him for no apparent reason. He was prepared anyway; it would not take him by surprise.

Five minutes later, he arrived at the Hotel Markesal. He went up to his room and turned on the light, letting himself to see from the window, before closing it and drawing the curtains. He checked that the room had searched again. Although, the microphone stayed in the same place. Inside the phone.

He did a new check sweep. Everything was as he left it. He turned off the light, locked the door with the chair on the desk. He showered, and before going to bed, observed through the small opening in the window curtains that Inspector Kustinov had gone.

He had no doubt that they were subjecting him to a harsh and
fierce surveillance. He was partly reassured, remembering that
no one knew why he had sent to the embassy of this country.

-oo0oo-

A RISKY DECISION

It was Sunday. The embassy was deserted. Only the policemen who were on duty remained inside the embassy, watching the outside of the building.

Jack went to the embassy with the excuse of putting and operational monitor, so as not to have display problems on normal working days.

Once inside, he scanned the surveillance monitors to find out the location of the police who were on duty inside the embassy. Everything was quiet and calm.

By mid-morning, he decides to carry out his plan.

Leave the surveillance room. He goes stealthily to the ambassador´s office. After opening the front door of the secretary´s office, he closes it inside so that he is not caught red-handed and goes yo the ambassador's one.

He sweeps with his watch, to check if there is any hidden microphone, through which secret information may be coming out, without the ambassador being aware.

He carefully checked where a device microphone could placed without seeing it, from any points of the office.

He sits in the ambassador's armchair and check that there is a ventilation grill on the opposite wall. It was a good place to put a video camera inside.

Disassemble the phone and the intercom, to check if there is any listening device. Everything is normal.

Turn the armchair to the right. Rest his hand on the side table. The hands of his watch rotated quickly and senselessly. He removes the watch and when he brings it closer to the table lock, the same movement occurs again.

Remove the lock on the extension table and inside there is a microchip. He extracts it with the utmost care and takes a photo of it with his mobile.

He immediately sends an encrypted message to his friend Paul Blanchard in Quantico, requesting that inform him of the characteristics of the microchip.

"I request urgent information about; this type of microchip, range and class of receiver that links to it.
Report using special key, 122JB."

Back in his surveillance control room, he puts operative the monitor of the video camera installed in the ambassador's office.

He was very pleased to check the camera was placed in the right possition, and recorded everything that moves inside. Now, it only remains to wait until the next shipment of the diplomatic pouch received.

When he finished his work, before coming out from the office, he lelf inoperative the camera in the ambassador's office and at the same time removed a piece from the starter, leaving the camera completely unusable. To avoid mistakes and unpleasant surprises.

However, till the next day, he woudn't receive news from the agency, reporting the characteristics of the microchip.

He only had, to wait.

A DANGEROUS GAME

When he leaves the embassy, he decides to go walking to the hotel. The afternoon invited for a walk. He wasn´t rush to get to hotel. He was deep in his thoughts.

Go past the bus stop. His sixth sense prevents him. In line, several people were waiting for the bus to arrive, including the secret police with the newspaper under the arm.

Suddenly he turns and stands in line, waiting his turn. When the bus arrives at the stop, people get on, keeping the order of the queue.

When the police officer was inside, Jack turns around. He does not get on the bus and it moves away. When the secret police noticed the maneuver, tried to get out, but the last people who have got on the bus, block the hallway. The bus started, leaving him nailed to his seat, with no possibility of getting off.

He curses mentaly the american a thousand times. His boss, inspector Kustinov, advised him of this move, but the american had played it without him noticing.

However, that would not mean that he would give up his efforts. He would get off at the next stop and go back. Until he finds the american again. He wanted to show him that no one was making fun of him.

But it wasn't going to be that easy. The American took a taxi from the bus stop to the hotel. From the taxi, he watched as the secret policeman returned on foot from the previous stop. Possibly, he thought he would meet the American on the way back.

He dined at the hotel restaurant. He got up from the table and just at moment coming in the restaurant the policeman with the newspaper under the arm.

-ooOoo-

Monday afternoon. Jack had taken surveillance, like a normal job. He was satisfied with the work done lately, since he posted to the embassy.

Suddenly, he felt a vibration in his left hand, it came from his wristwatch. The display advised from a message received. He touched the screen and the following message displayed:

"The lock microphone is highly sophisticated of the latest generation. It emits in a band of 480 Mhz. Automatically eliminates interference. It reaches a distance, between eighty to one hundred and twenty meters. Due to its size, it could placed on a fountain pen, a button, a pin, a brooch or anywhere else, even in an ashtray.

These devices connected to a high precision digital receiver. They are usually the size of a packet of tobacco. It is so sophisticated that its capacity can be expanded by up to sixty spy microphones or wiretapping within the same receiver. Good luck, Jack."

Upon knowing the message, he felt a great desire to continue the search. Now he felt very happy, he had managed to find the tip of the skein. Now, it's just a matter of pulling patiently, until reaching the skein.

He touched the command "to save", and sent it to a folder where he would have it at his disposal. It would be ready to be used in the future, if necessary. Possibly some people would receive a nasty surprise.

The next day, it would submitted to a close surveillance on the three most important people in the embassy; Mr. Harrelson, his secretary Miss Donalson, and Mr. Sieman.

-oo0oo-

THE INSPECTOR IGOR KUSTINOV
AND THE AGENT GREGORZ MALENKO

He arrived at the embassy thirty minutes before his working time.

After on-call control, Jack immediately heads to the offices of police Chief Kenneth Diaz. Officer who is in charge of the security control of the embassy and the personnel.

The office door was open. Jack went in without knocking. In the first office, there are two police officers working at their table.

- What do you want, Mr. Brown? -- He says, after checking his name on the identification plate -- Can I help you?

- I wish to speak to your boss, Lieutenant Kosher. – Jack, also identifies him by his badge.

- Well, Mr. Brown. What is the matter?

- Tell him, I want to talk to him. Only that. It is urgent!

- Very well, Mr. Brown, wait a moment.

Knock on the back door. A strong and authoritative voice is heard, answering from behind the door.

- Come in!

- Sir, a certain Mr. Brown wishes to speak with you. He says is urgent.

- Well, tell him to come in. I hope he don't give me the joke, I'm not for nonsense. These office workers made a mountain of anything. They see ghosts where there are none.

The lieutenant gestures for him to access his boss's office.

Personally, they don´t know each other. Chief Kenneth looks puzzled when he checks the identity card. In front of him, there is a person whom he had never seen before in the embassy compound. But he carried the card that identifies him, as an employee.

His position obliged to, Chief Kenneth to know and have the identity file for the embassy personnel.

- Come in and sit down, please. -- Meanwhile searches in the inbox the document. Among them, find an envelope. He opens it and inside there is an internal statement, which informs him about the registration the new employee. -- Well, Mr. Brown. What is the honour your visit?

Jack, take a good look at the man sitting behind the desk in the office. From his appearance, seemed to be of Puerto Rican origin, with dark complexion, but not black. He looked sixty years old, tall with a strong constitution. For his haircut, his workmanship and his behavior, he had no doubt that he was a marine.

Kenneth did the same, analyzed the man in front of him. Brown, in his fifties, apparently was not as tall or as strong as he was, but could be say, he was in good shape.

- Chief Kenneth. My name is Jack Brown. I've been assigned to this embassy to cover a casualty in the surveillance control room. The reason for my visit is to inform you that since my arrival, two secret policemen have followed me. From the embassy to the Markesol hotel where I have a room reserved and back to the embassy. I have observed them for several days. There are days that alternate in their surveillance and monitoring.

- Mr. Brown, are you sure? It may be a coincidence, many often, you usualy meet many people who come and go from their work daily.

- Excuse me, chief. This is not the first time that I have assigned to an embassy, and as you know, we have received instructions on how we should behave. Also, I feel his gaze on my neck when they look at me, even with my back turned.

- Mister Brown. Have you been disturbed at any time?

- No, I have not. But I suppose you will have a security file on the police and agents of this country, particularly, those who move freely in this city, I mean secret agents.

From the safety box, he takes out several folders containing detailed information, about police and secret agents.

Jack takes his time, checking detailed through the files with their corresponding photos.

In the first folder, he cannot find the police photos.

In the second folder, a couple of sheets were about to finish reviewing them, when on the penultimate sheet were the photos of the two agents. He takes out the two sheets with the informations, which correspond to each of the agents, who follow him.

- These two are the two agents, who follow me so closely, that sometimes, they seem to be friends of mine. A couple of days ago, I almost tripped over this one. -- He pointed to the photo on the file. – When leaving the cafeteria.

- This is Inspector Igor Kustinov. A bad person, even his fellows fear him. This other whom you almost stumbled upon, his name is Gregorz Malenko and he is the subordinate of Kustinov. Normally, the latter is known by the nickname of the "butcher", so that, you can get an idea of the nickname. They are two of the worst types that you usually find.

- Well, I will be careful.

 - For your safety and peace of mind, Mr. Brown. If you want, I can give you protection.

- No, now I just wanted to know who they were. Now I feel partly calm. I take care of these people. I mean, now I know their names. I will consider them. So far, I have ignored them. I'll keep pretending to be distracted, as I haven't noticed. Thanks chief for your help. Now, I go back to my job.

Kenneth watched him quietly leave his office. He was surprised not to notice the slightely bit of fear in Mr. Brown face, when he informed him of who they were. Another in his place would not have hesitated to ask for protection.

-ooOoo0-

Jack kept an eye on what Mr. Sieman was doing. He worked writing down the documents in the ledger. Finished the notes, he opened the drawer of his table, to keep it inside the aforementioned book. It was only a moment, but he saw inside the desk drawer a pack of "Bison" cigarettes. American blond tobacco. What surprised Jack is that he had never seen him smoke, not even with a cigarette in his mouth.

There was little time left to finish the workday. He decided not to stop watching Mr. Sieman. However, with the video camera he tried to search if there was an ashtray in the office. He swept the entire compound and couldn't find it, or at least it wasn't in sight.

At the end of the working day, the staff left the building. Half an hour later, only Jack and the police on duty remained in the building, watching the embassy.

He waited half an hour, to be sure, that all the administrative staff had gone. Then, turned off the monitor of Mr. Sieman´s office, so that his entrance to the office would not record.

Mr. Sieman locked his office door, following the instructions of the security protocol imposed by the embassy.

Jack made use of his multiuse scout knife, using the picklock like a key. He opened the office door without forcing it. He closed it once inside.

He had to use the picklock again to open the lock on the table drawer. He carefully pulled out its contents, putting on the table. He was looking for the receiver, the one hidden in the simulated pack of Bisonte cigarettes, and the Harley Davidson pen, in its cap would have a listening microchip.

He did not need to get his watch too close to the receiver, so that the hands began to rotate randomly. He looked for the pen, but it was not in the drawer of the table. He took a photo with his mobile phone and kept in its memory.

With all these evidences, he had more than enough to unmask Mr. Sieman and send him to prison, but he was sure that more people were involved in this matter.

Jack placed back everything taken out in the same position as were in the drawer. He closed and left the office. He got rid of the latex gloves he was wearing, so as not to leave any traces. He put them in the bag in his locker.

-oo0oo-

The days passed, like those of the previous week, in the most complete calm. Surveillance was boring and tedious. Jack waited impatiently for the day of the arrival of the diplomatic valise.

Meanwhile, from time to time he would put the surveillance camera in the ambassador's office into operation. He wanted to be sure that when the time came he wouldn't let him down. He had risked too much. If something went wrong he would have to wait another week.

-oo0oo-

THE VALUABLE DIPLOMATIC POUCH

At last, the day so desired by Jack arrived. It was none other than, the day of the arrival of the diplomatic valise.

Jack connects the video camera installed in the ambassador's office. It works perfectly; turn it off until it is time to use it.

Meanwhile, he is still watching and waiting for the arrival of the diplomatic pouch, through Mr. Sieman's camera.

Half morning. Sergeant Joe McCrea hands it over to Mr. Sieman. This signed the receipt with the pen; he had in his vest pocket.

Jack was surprised that he did not use one of those cheap Bic Cristal pens that he had in his pencil box, and that all the employees of official bodies usually use economically.

Jack took advantage of that moment to attract the pen with the zoom of the monitor. He was not surprised to see that it was a Harley Davidson brand pen.

Due to the type of pen, it had enough capacity to house a listening microfilm inside its cap. He put the pen in the top pocket of his jacket.

Then he placed the diplomatic valise in the document delivery cart. He left his office, closing behind him.

He took the pouch to Miss Donalson, who, was in charge of taking it to the ambassador, who would be in charge of opening it by means of a special key, which only he possessed.

Jack connected the camera. He checked as the ambassador, proceeded to open the diplmatic pouch. Once opened the ambassador took out the mail. Miss Blanca Donalson classified them.

Once the contents of the puch have emptied, the ambassador proceeded to read each of the letters, and endorsed them later, before delivered to Mr. Sieman, for distribution to the different office departments.

The ambassador opened the letters in front of Miss Donalson, except one, a sealed brown envelope, which indicated, "Top Secret & Confidential". This kept unopened in the safebox by the ambassador.

All the comments made, during the time they were distributing the mail, was clearly picked up by the microphone that Mr. Sieman carried in the upper pocket of his jacket and from this, to the receiver that he had in his office.

Mr. Sieman waited patiently in Miss Donalson's office, waiting for the documents for distribution. After the delivery of the mail is completed, Mr. Harrelson remains inside his office for the rest of the morning.

Jack watches him. He was immersed in his work. However, Mr. Harrelson was thoughtful and nervous. He had repeatedly looked at his wristwatch.

His intuition told him that something was going to happen sooner than later. He knew the human behaviors. During his twenty-five years as an agent, he had treated with countless people of all social classes. The ambassador's movements were not normal.

-oo0oo-

THE EVIDENCE

At the end of the morning, the ambassador opens the safebox, and takes out the sealed brown envelope. It remained sealed. He kept it in his handbag.

Through the intercom, the amabssador asks his secretary that the embassy driver wait for him in half an hour in the courtyard of the embassy. He will be away for about an hour.

Jack didn't expect to have this difficulty. An unexpected, serious and difficult problem presented itself. Leaving the embassy was not going to be so easy, but he had no choice but to follow him. He had to find out where he was going with the brown envelope.

Without thinking twice, he leaves the video camera in the ambassador's office recording. He turns off the monitor and walks out the back door. The police officer who was on duty greets him, while Jack ran his card through the scanner.

He disappears from the view of the outdoor surveillance camera. Around the street, stops a taxi and tells the taxi driver to wait in front of the American Embassy.

The taxi driver was not surprised. It was not the first time that followed other car. It had been a long time since he had not involved in a follow-up career. The longer it took the wait, the more he would charge for the service.

Ten minutes of waiting, and the ambassador's car appears.

Jack tells the taxi driver to follow the ambassador car at a certain distance, without losing sight of him. They reached the northern part of the city. The car stopped at a bookshop, the Libreríe La Patrie. The ambassador enters with his briefcase.

Ten minutes later, he leaves the bookshop. He had a book in his hand and the briefcase.

He gets in the car and returns to the embassy.

Jack leaves the taxi driver, paying him the amount of the service. One of his forebodings came to mind, and he wanted to see if he was right.

He entered a costume shop, opposite the bookshop. He bought a military Saharan, and the typical cap with a visor, both gray, a wig, a false white beard, and a folding cane.

He went into the fitting room, changing clothes, disguising himself as an old man. When he came out of the fitting room, the clerk rubbed his eyes at the sight of him. He didn´t believe the transformation made by his client.

 - Excuse me, if I have amazed you. That shows that my costume is good. I want to give a suprise to good friend. When I saw your store, the idea occurred to me.

He put the lothes in a bag and left the store. At about the same time, Inspector Igor Kustinov came out of the La Patrie bookshop, accompanied by his hound, Gregorz Malenko, stuffing an envelope into his inner jacket pocket. Now he was sure that his intuition had not failed him.

They crossed the street, and entered a bar. They asked for a jug of beer. When Jack walked in, they were in lively chat. He sat at the table next to them, a meter away. He couldn't hear what they were talking about, in a low voice barely audible. Although sometimes they seemed to say something funny, which made them laugh aloud.

One of the comments made, he thought to hear Harrelson's name. However, he couldn't hear anything else. They kept mumbling under their breath. Gregorz occasionally glanced around him, as if making sure they couldn't hear them, nor the old man sitting at the next table. They did not care of.

The old man was bent over the table with an empty glass in his right hand. Soon he would be drunk as a vat. He had had three glasses of vodca, and had ordered another glass. He would end up sleeping the drunkeness in the bar, or sitting on the bench in a plaza, or lying down on the floor in any dirty alley.

Not long after, the two policemen left. At the exit of the bar, before saying goodbye, they spent a few minutes in animated talk. Each one went off on different paths.

The old man paid for the drinks, and leaning on his cane, he left the bar, chanting from one side to the other. The few clients, who were there, looked at each other to seeing the amount of vodca the old man have drunk. They paid no more attention to him; they were accustomed to see lonely old men, without family taking refuge in vodka to forget their pains or loneliness.

-ooOoo-

Jack needed to get back to the embassy. He took the opportunity to go into other department stores, and change clothes in the toilets.

He hailed a taxi, which took him to the back of the embassy. He entered without problem. The police officers controlling the embassy entrance had changed. His entry, although it would controlled, twice perhaps would go unnoticed, if not, he would take care of finding any excuse.

Later, when he was looking forward to the surveillance room, to find out what had happened to the envelope. He turned on the monitor of the amabassador office. He was sitting and dictating several letters to Miss Donalson. It was about to strike six in the afternoon.

Minutes before the departure time, Miss Donalson returned with the signature folder with the typed letters that the ambassador had previously dictated to her.

Once signed by the ambassador, she put the letters in their envelopes. Then the secretary calls Mr. Sieman, to collect and send them by mail. She left the office, but not before saying goodbye to the ambassador.

The ambassador, stayed in his office a few minutes, until he was sure the staff of the embassy had left the building. Then took the brown briefcase out from a drawer in his desk, to keep in the save deposit box.

Jack turn off the monitor and save the recording. His mission was about to end.

The evidences admitted no doubt.

-ooOoo-

He was resting in his room. Lying on the bed. He was slow to get to sleep.

The night made him too long. He had barely sleeped for about three hours. The rest of the night spent tossing and turning in bed. He was eager for dawn. He thought that possibly it would all be over in a few days. Mr. Harrelson once confessed.

He got up earlier than usual. He had a good shower to clear his ideas. It was the first time that, he would forced to question an ambassador, who enjoyed great prestige and consideration, before the government and among his colleagues.

He went down to the hotel cafeteria and had a hearty breakfast. He didn't know what the rest of the day might bring him.

He was walking out the door of the cafeteria when the secret police Gregorz Malenko entered. They are face to face. Jack, don't give him the way. They stare at each other, waiting for the other to move. Jack don't intend to give way. Thought. Let him out before entering, courtesy of good manners.

- Sorry sir. -- Said police Malenko, reluctantly giving him way.

- Thank you. -- He answers him with a gesture, not with a smile out of courtesy.

-ooOoo-

JACK IDENTIFIES HIMSELF AS AGENT

Jack went to the embassy earlier than usual. After the control, he goes directly to the office of Chief Kenneth Díaz. The door was open. He came in without knocking. Lieutenant Josué Kosher greets him. He got up to receive him.

- Good morning, Mr. Brown. May I help you?

- Good morning, Lieutenant. I need to speak to chief Kenneth Diaz.

- Wait a moment, Mr. Brown. I will let you know that you are here.

He didn´t have time to knock on the door of his chief´s office when he appeared through the door.

- Thank you, lieutenant. I heard that Mr. Brown wanted to speak to me. Please come in and sit down. Tell me how I can help you!

- I'll tell you right now. Please close the door and listen me carefully. The conversation we are going to have is highly confidential and secret.

 Chief Kenneth looks at the person sitting in front of him with surprise.

- I am a special agent of the government. I belong to the GSSS. (Special Secret Government Service). They sent me from Quantico Agency. We are aware secret documents are leaked to this country through this embassy. They sent me to solve this problem. -- Chief Kenneth cannot believe what´s hearing. It is impossible. I hope, he's not crazy, he thought. -- I know it's hard to believe. I follow. No one, not even the ambassador himself, knows who I am, except you. If you have doubts about me, send a message to this address, today, referring to me. -- He gives him a note with a special key. -- You will receive instructions immediately on this matter.

- You have no doubt that I will verify what you tell me, Mr. Brown. As you know, I have to fulfill with the protocol.

- Chief Kenneth. ¡Do it! I would appreciate it if you would send it out today. Possibly tomorrow will be late. I will need your services, even before I get the answer. Please don't delay. We'll be in touch.

He left the office, leaving him intrigued. He didn´t have hardly time to redo the surprise. He couldn't believe what he had told him. He would never have imagined that such a thing could happen at the embassy. It was under his surveillance.

Since assigned him as chief of service, three years ago, he had never had a problem. Except for some small incidents with anti-American groups, which did the same police in the country quickly dissolved. It could said that everything had passed peacefully.

Nevertheless, he would find out who Mr. Brown really was, and if what he had told him was true. To heal in health, he sent two messages. One to the GSSS. to collect information from the agency and another to his superior chief in Washington, asking information on this matter. He would be waiting for instructions. If the leaks were true, he wanted his back well covered. The matter was difficult to solve.

-ooOoo-

MAXIMUM PRIORITY

The next day, Chief Kenneth Díaz arrives at his office. Lt. Josué Kosher was in the office. As usual, he greets him and goes to the coffee maker, to serve himself a cup of coffee.

He hadn't finished his cup of coffee, when opens the computer and checks the received e-mails in the inbox. Two stand out, attracting his attention.

He did not expect to receive such a quick response from the GSSS Agency, which says:

"Agent Jack Brown. Lend him any service or help for him requested. ¡Take good note, any service! If he need funds, please provide them." Delete from your computer, this e-mail, once red it, highly confidential!

The second message, received from his superior chief. It left him any possibility to doubt:

"Undercover Special Agent of the Government. Maximum collaboration. Lend him maximum cooperation. Provide him whatever he needs without consulting. Special orders."

There was no longer any doubt; something was simmering inside the embassy. Someone was leaking secret information, without anyone noticing.

As chief of surveillance, he was concerned about the news. He knew all the employees and all the confidential staff reports were excellent. They had been exhaustively selected.

He took a copy of the personnel files out of the safety box, to review them, and have again a look, carefully at each one in case he could get any conclusions, about the person or persons, who could be involved in the leak of documents.

-ooOoo-

The day passed, without news of Jack Brown. He knew he was working in the surveillance control room. He input on his computer. He would be pending until the last minute, in case he needed his services.

The workday was about to end. Suddenly the phone at chief Kenneth Diaz's desk rings.

- Here Kenneth. Tell me?

- I'm Jack. See you in half an hour, in your office. -- He did not give him time to answer, when he had already hung up.

After half an hour, steps heard and stopped in front of Chief Kenneth's. Then there is a knock on the door.

- Go ahead, Jack. Come in.

- Good afternoon, Kenneth. I suppose you will have received news from my agency.

- Yes sir. I received one from your agency and another from my superior chief. I wanted to heal myself in health. This matter is very delicate and I don't want to be involved more than necessary. However, I am at your disposal.

- You do very well. I should have acted the same way. Well from now on. I need your collaboration. I will tell you that my work, since my arrival, has based on reviewing the tapes of the last three months. Now, I have gathered enough evidence to unmask who are implicated in this matter.

- Excuse me Jack, that's completely impossible. I explain you. Scarcely a month ago, following the protocol established by the government, for the embassies established abroad, I made a complete checking. The verification gave negative.

- Well, Kenneth, I don't question your work. But, as I said, I have gathered enough evidences to show you that I am right.

- I suppose your evidences will verified.

- Yes. They are and I have them. But I want it to be done in your presence, and with the ambassador, Mr Harrelson. So we have to meet as soon as possible, to cut the leak of documents. I think this afternoon at last time would be a good idea when the staff leaves the embassy.

- Excuse me, Jack. I think it is too hasty. Maybe the ambassador is not available.

- Tell the ambassador, that this is an urgent matter, concerning to the surveillance of the embassy. That there is a listening microchip in his office.

- Please Jack, don't overdo it. I think you are exaggerating the situation. I cannot believe it. That is impossible!

- Just do what I tell you. I have not sent for sightseeing. Everything will clarified this afternoon. Quote him in your office. Not in the ambassador's one.

-ooOoo-

THE CONFESSION

It is eight o'clock in the evening. Jack just made his shift change. His partner Patrick Riarson took his place in the surveillance room.

He walked straight to the chief security office. Who was waiting for him in the company of the ambassador, Mr. Harrelson. Both were serious and circumspect.

Then, from previous greetings, Jack takes the word.

- Sir Ambassador, first I want to inform you, that I am a GSSS agent from the government agency. I have been sent, to cut the bleeding and discover the people who are taking out secrets documents from this embassy, which consequences are unpredictables, due the its contents.

- I hope, Mr Brown, you know the seriousness of what you are talking about. I guess you know what you tells.

- Sir, I have many years of service, I know what I tell myself and what I do. I can show you that a microchip has installed in your office. I have asked Chief Kenneth to come with me as a witness until this matter is over.

- If you are so sure, I want you to prove it to me with facts. Otherwise, I would be obliged to take you leave with charges, for raising false testimonies.

- Mr Harrelson, let's go to your office, but I warn you that we must remain silent, since everything we talk about will be recorded on a receiver that's also inside this building. Your conversations and calls, ambassador, will have recorded and listened to, for about three months.

Neither could believe what Jack told them. Chief Kenneth was increasingly reluctant to admit what agent Brown says. But, he speaks to them with such assurance and conviction that he was taking charge of the gravity of what is happening.

They moved to the ambassador's office. Jack remembered them to remain silent. He sat down in the armchair of the table and turned to the right, towards the extra table. He signals them to come closer.

Then, he brings his watch closer to the lock on the small extra table the watch hands begin to spin rapidly meaningless. He pulls it out and brings it up repeatedly, the hands turn over and again.

Jack takes out of his pocket, the scout multi-purpose knife. Use one of its pieces as a picklock. Open the lock and take it apart. Inside there was a listening microchip.

To the amazement of the ambassador and the chief of police, Jack puts it back inside it, and mounts the lock in the drawer of the utility table.

They leave the office in silence, returning to Chief Kenneth's office.

- Well, ambassador. What do you tell me now, am I right or not? -- The ambassador was completely blocked, he didn't know what to say. He remained quiet. – Now, answer me this question. Do you remember any repairs carried out recently in your office?

- Let me see. -- He thought for a few seconds. -- I remember about three months ago, a new lock was replaced it again.

- Let me tell you, since that date, they have been listening to you and recording all your conversations, you had in this office.

Next, he showed them the information received by their Agency, regarding the microchip:

"The microphone place in the lock is highly sophisticated, the latest generation. It emits in a band of 480 MHz. And eliminates interferences automatically. It reaches a distance, between eighty to one hundred and twenty meters. Due to its size, this can place it on a fountain pen, on a button, on a pin, or anywhere else, even in an ashtray.

These devices normally connected to a high precision digital receiver. They are usually the size of a packet of tobacco. It is so sophisticated that up to sixty spy wiretap microchips within the same receiver can expand its capacity.
Good luck, Jack."

- Well. Then, why didn't you destroy the microchip when you took it out of the lock?

- If I destroy it, they will realize that we have found it, and we will not catch the person, who has the receiver.

- If this is all, I will retire. I feel tired. I suppose you will keep me informed the progresses of the investigation. – Said the ambassador.

- Yes sir, I will inform you right now, if you don't leave. I have not finished yet. I have more evidences that you will like to know them. May I use your video player, Kenneth?

- Yes, please use it.

Kenneth, insert the recorded tape into the video player. He makes it on and the photo of the lock with the microchip inside it appears.

Then, the message received from its Quantico offices appears, with the analysis of it.

The recording tape shows the route of the embassy pouch, from Mr. Sieman's office to Miss Donalson's office. The tape returns to the second recording in Sieman's office. In which it shows the Harley Davidson pen cap with another microchip and the receiver camouflaged in a packet of Bisonte brand cigarettes.

- Good work Mr. Brown, now we know the person that leaks the documents. What are you waiting for, to arrest him?

- Simply, because there is another person, who is actually removing out the documents.

- That's not can be. The documents are kept in the safety box of the embassy. There has never been a robbery, it would be impossible. I'm the only person who has access to the savety box.

- I know that sir. Let me introduce you to the last part of my research. I think it is the most interesting. You will love to see it for yourself.

Recording begins with the delivery of the diplomatic pouch by Sergeant Joe McCrea to Mr. Sieman. The recording tape followed the way to the pouch. Until was handed over to Miss Donalson, and the entrance to the ambassador's office.

The tape-recorded, all the movements between the ambassador and his secretary Miss Donalson, who would take in charge of classifying the correspondence. The tape-recorded, the moment the ambassador puts the unopened envelope in the safety box.

Later, it´s observed as the ambassador takes out the brown envelope from the safety box and puts it in his briefcase. Leaving the office minutes later.

The final part of the recording shows how the ambassador come to his office and puts in the envelope in the safety box.

Mr. Harrelson was in shock. He was livid and could barely pronounce a word. Who and how had introduced a video camera in his office, without asking him permission. It´s prohibited without authorization.

- I remind you, Mr. Brown, that this tape is not valid. It has placed in my office without my   authorization. I will take legal action against you and will use the weight of the law to put you in prison, until you get rotten

- Mr. Harrelson. Calm down! I am not your enemy. Please don't say sonsenses. I have placed the video camera, with the powers given by my agency. Right now, you have the power that I want to give you. None!

- I shall take the necessary measures to protect myself.

 - Chief Kenneth, detain him and take him into custody in his rooms at the embassy. That is an order.

- I'm sorry, sir. I have received instructions from Washington to put myself under the orders of Mr. Brown. I really feel what have happened you. But the situation puts me on the side of the law.

- This is all a lie, it is a hoax perpetrated by Mr. Brown, who was sent for the purpose of disqualifying and disgracing me.

- Sir. Watch this video.

He puts the recording on, when he took his briefcase out of his desk drawer and put it in the safety box.

- Have you observed anything abnormal, Kenneth?

Kenneth remains thoughtful without answering. Jack realized that something is escaping him. The most important part goes unnoticed. Replay the recording.

Jack watches as Kenneth tries to do his best to pay the utmost attention to the recording, but continues inadvertently refer to it. Rewind the tape back again, and for the recording, now the ambassador puts the envelope in the safety box.

- Okay, Kenneth I'm going to explain you. See when he takes the envelope out of the safety box. -- He stops the zooms on it. -- As you can see, the envelope is closed. Now, see when he returns it to deposit in the savety box. - He does the same operation. -- The envelope has been unsealed and opened, and surely, its contents photocopied in La Patrie Bookshop.

The ambassador was puzzled. How did Jack know, that he had been in La Patrie Bookshop? He showed him a photo leaving the bookstore and with a book in the hand, getting into the embassy car.

- Now, I suppose it is very clear, who is the person, who is selling and passing secrets documents to our enemies. -- Jack tells him. -- Or do you have any doubts. Sir, ambassador?
Kenneth, remain incredulous. He could't believe it. He had been three years at the embassy. He felt a great affection for

Mr. Harrelson, whom considered a good person, and a great professional. He would have given the life for him without thinking. He couldn't believe that for money was selling secrets to the Belarusians.

Jack realizes the moment that Kenneth was going through. With encountered feelings. Always, he had considered him for an honest and just man. But, the evidence hinted the opposite of what he thought. He was, morally sunk and in a sea of doubts.

Mr. Harrelson came from a wealthy family and from several generations of illustrious politicians. He didn't think the ambassador did it for money. Since the ambassador divorced, he barely left the embassy. Just to attend parties and official meetings that requested his presence, as ambassador.

- Friend Kenneth, I am sorry, but I have to take a statement from Mr. Harrelson. Despite your appreciation for him, you will have to put under arrest at the embassy, until I could send him back home. As soon as I send the report to the Agency, and they give me the instructions, to follow.

- No please. That's not, for God's sake! -- He screamed desperately, collapsed between sobs. He hid his face between his hands. -- You cannot do that. If you send me back home, they will kill my father.

- Who is going to kill your father? Explain yourself better. -- Jack asked.

Without raising his head, holding it between his hands, as if wanting to hide the shame of his actions, he confesses:

- "Four months ago, my father paid me a visit. Since leaving his position in the Senate, along with my mother, he was planning a trip to Paris and other countries in Europe. It was the great illusion of their lives. However, before making the trip, my mother fell ill, and soon after, she died.

When I assigned me to this embassy, before he got depressed, my sister and I encouraged him to make the trip, which would take advantage of to visit me, since I was in Europe.

He did so. I had him for two weeks with me. When we said goodbye, due to my work, I couldn't accompany to take him leave to the airport. I gave concrete instructions to my driver to help him with the luggage and to wait until the flight had taken off. My driver never lost sight of him.

When we said goodbye at the embassy, we agreed that as soon as he got home, he made me a call; I wanted to be sure that he had gotten home safely.

A couple of days went by without hearing news from my father. His behavior was not normal. I phoned my sister if she had news. She said me he had not arrived. She thought, he was still with me. Fact that suprised me. My father used to be very methodical in everything he did during his life.

I started making inquiries about where he could be. First with the airline. They informed that he appeared on the boarding list. For what had left the country.

I tried to find out, by all means, where he could be. I contacted with the arrival control at London airport. They informed that have not record of his arrival. Nor did he appear on any of the companies' boarding lists, which served from London to New York JFK. Airport, Newark or Washington Dulles Airport.
I was desperated; I did not know what to do or who to turn to. Everything was contradictory.

I had been looking for clues for a week that could lead me to my father's whereabouts, when suddenly I received a phone call. They informed me that they have my father in their possession. I understood they had kidnapped. In exchange for his life, they asked me to provide them with classified and secret information about the location of the nuclear bases that our goverment were establishing with our allied countries in Europe, in exchange for the life of my father.

Days later, I receive a personal and confidential letter, in which they send me a photo of my father alive, in a horrible cell sitting on a three-legged stool. I was at a terrible crossroads. For a few days, I hesitated between choosing my father or my country. I preferred to save his life, although deep down, I knew that when they didn't need me, they would kill him. I chose him. You must understand he´s my father!

I did not know how they found out the day of the arrival of the embassy pouch, much less, how they knew the arrival of the secret documents. Now, I understand it, from the microchip in the lock.

Mr. Brown, I put myself in your hands, I will do whatever you ask, but please do not send me home, I do not want anything to happen to my father.

The resolution of the case had become complicated. Jack meditated for a few minutes. He studied mentally and carefully the difficult situation, which he had suddently had before him.

- Well, for now this is our secret. Nobody must know it. We cannot put at risk your father's life. By this, I mean that you, sir, must continue working as before. You have to leave the microchip listening. Otherwise, they´ll realize that something is wrong, and they can get rid of their father. As for you, Kenneth, tomorrow I will meet in your office.

Then he gos to Mr. Harrelson, to give him instructions.

- Mr Harrelson, from this moment on and for the time of this investigation, we´ll not be in contact, unless an unforeseen event arises. Either way, you´ll receive direct information through Chief Kenneth. I want you to know that, since my arrival I´m closely watched by the police of this country. I do not want any mistake to fail the rescue that I have to carry out, for the liberation of your father. Kenneth, see you tomorrow.

Without anything else, he ended the meeting.

-ooOoo-

JACK, THE MAN

It was Sunday, noon. Jack had the day off. He decided to walk. He left the hotel. He would take advantage of his free time, to visit and know "in situ", all those streets and shops, and stop in front of those shop windows, the ones he saw when traveling daily on the public bus, from the hotel to the embassy and back.

There was a large influx of public, strolling through the streets, avenues and squares, where children played in the small playgrounds, while their parents watched them sitting on stone benches. The bars and restaurants were practically full.

Halfway, he entered a restaurant where found a couple of empty tables. He didn´t doubt it. He sat in one of them. It didn't take long for the waiter to appear, who carried him the menus card wrote in Russian. It was not an obstacle he knew the language perfectly. Among other things, it was one of the reasons, why was sent to Minsk.

He requested his preferred menu, number five; a cutlet with fried potatoes, accompanied by a mug of beer, dessert apple pie and coffee.

After lunch, initially his idea was to return to the hotel to rest. He thought it better and changed his mind. He had appointed with Chief Kenneth on Monday morning. He had the day off and all night to think.

He had not been walking for long, when suddenly found himself in the center of the city, in front of the Cathedral of Holy Spirit. He approaches its portal from which the characteristic smell of incense and burnt wax comes out. It was open until late afternoon.

Without trying, attracted by curiosity, when he realizes he was inside. Despite not being a very usual time, inside the cathedral there were a large number of parishioners praying. The gloom, the characteristic smell of incense and burnt wax that floated in the air of the Sacred Enclosure enveloped him with a special fate.

He sat in the last row of the bench that was free. He didn´t go unnoticed that most of the people in the central nave were elderly. The submission of the dictatorship and the difficulties of daily life, made them take refuge in prayer, to continue having strength, and continue forward.

The noise produced by the whisper of the prayer of the parishioners, most of whom were seatted in the central nave, invited silence and recollection. At the head of the central nave, its baroque-style High Altar was imposing due to its beauty. In the center of it, preside over an icon of incalculable value; that of the Mother of God venerated and loved by all the Belarusian people.

Jack stood motionless for a moment, admiring its interior. The wealth gathered inside, it was differed from the poverty of many of the parishioners there prostrated and their inhabitants. Most of the parishioners had nothing and sometimes that nothing; they donated it in the charity boxes, for their Church!

Without realizing him, in that Sacred Enclosure, he felt an inner peace and the need to prostrate himself on knees, pleading the Mother of God, for his family and for his wife Claudia, whom he remember her lovely.

Before leaving the Cathedral, asked the Mother of God for one last request. To help him on this mission, to finish it, as soon as possible, and help him to rescue alive a good person, without having to use violence, to avoid having victims involved.

-ooOoo-

From the cathedral to the hotel there was almost an hour walking. He passed the bus stop. He was so engrossed in his thoughts that had left the bus stop, behind without realizing it.

The sound of the horn of a vehicle returned him to reality. Someone tried to cross the avenue, not using the crosswalk.

He was hungry. He looked at the time on his wristwatch. It was seven thirty in the afternoon. Time had passed by flying inside the cathedral and walking through to the hotel. It was a good time for dinner.

He went into the Mirtov Restaurant, halfway between the embassy and the hotel. He picked up the menu card from the table. He asked for menu number ten. It was a very similar menu to number five, which ordered at the hotel restaurant.

As they served them, he sipped sip after sip with delight, from the cold beer in the jug. He was in the mood and thirsty.

After dinner, continue on foot to the hotel. Before arriving, he stops at the shoe store´s window to browse the shoes on display. Note as if someone is watching him. It was the silhouette of the secret agent, Gregorz Malenko, standing on the opposite sidewalk with the newspaper under his arm. His figure reflected in the windowpanes.

Jack thought to himself, either they are too bad at their vigilance or the opposite, they don´t care that they know they are exercising a harsh vigilance, to put pressure on the person

95

on the person being watched. Jack was perfectly familiar with the methods imployed by these individuals. They abused by feeling strongly protected, for the simple fact of having a police badge.

Jach wasn't afraid of them. He was ready, to act at any time.

-oo0oo-

Monday. The sky had dawned a clear blue, and clear of clouds. When Jack entered the embassy, Chief Kenneth was waiting for him in his office.

- Good morning, Kenneth.

- Good morning, Mr. Brown.

- As you know, I closely watched by the two secret policemen; Inspector Igor Kustinov and his lapdog Gregorz Malenko. There is one very important thing to keep in mind. No, we want you to notice any change on our part, it would be fatal for Mr. Harrelson's father. We have to walk with leaden feet. I am sure they know much more than we suppose. They have to be involved in this matter.

They watch me, because in reality, don't know who I am. They don't have my file in their records. So, they don't really know if I'm an embassy employee or an agent. Since they kidnapped Mr Harrelson, as there has not been an official movement by the embassy, they considered safe themselves. So we must take advantage of this circumstance, and act quickly in secret and with great caution.

96

- If you want anything, you only have to tell me, you know that I am at your disposal, Mr. Brown.

- Yes, I need five things. The first. Let us leave the protocol and we call each other by our names in one way or another we are partners. We are in the same matter. -- Kenneth, thanked him for the confidence with a gesture. -- The second, from tomorrow I will have full freedom of movement, so I will not attend my service in the surveillance room any more. Third. I want to know, if among your staff, there is any boy trained enough to help me on this mission. He must know that exist a great risk and that his life will be in danger if accept it. Fourth. A need a car with full confidence driver, at my complete disposal and he does not ask any questions. Fifth. I need half a million rubles at my disposal. Please let the ambassador know. Any comments regarding this matter must be out of the microchip's listening range. Keep this in mind when you are in the ambassador's office. Remember that any slip can cost the ambassador´s father life.

Kenneth took note of all the matters he asked him. He made no objection. Although, the amount required was of some importance, and did not require authorization, he had already received in advance; He, he had to provide, whatever he needed."

When he was alone, Kenneth thought, who is realy this guy called himself Jack Brown? Kenneth knew that it was not his real name, that he was using it as a cover. He was not a normal agent. He ordered and commanded without hesitation. He asked for half a million rubles, like the one he asks for a beer.

He was so intrigued to know the true personality of this guy, that he tried to get his file out of the secret government files, but it did not appear in any of them. So intrigued was he, that he tried to achieve it by other means.

He even tried to access the secret files of the GSSS Agency. He could not access, always got the same answer. "Denied. Does not exist. Please don't insist."

-oo0oo-

THE SEARCH BEGINS

The workday begins first time in the morning. It's eight o'clock. Jack came into the office of the Chief, Kenneth Díaz.

- Good morning, Kenneth. I hope you got me the required services.

- Good morning, Jack. Close the door. I think I have you what you need. -- He tells him:

- Good morning, Kenneth. I hope you have got me the required services.

Third. - Among my men, I have a young boy, clever and very well prepared. His parents are Russian of Jewish origin. He was born in Riga, so he speaks Russian perfectly and have my full confidence. You already know him. Lieutenant Josué Kosher. He worked at the Israeli embassy for a couple of years. He is not afraid of anything and is cold like ice. When he was eighteen years old, his parents immigrated to Israel. Mosad trained him. I think you know him. You will not find a better element.

The fourth. - ¿Do you remember the taxi driver, who picked you up at the airport upon arrival? His name is Nikolay Ivanov. He has too my full confidence. You can ask him how much help you need. Jack, believe me! Any help. He will be made available to you immediately, as son as you indicate it.

Fifth. - In the safety box of the embassy, the requested money is ready.

- Well. About your man, tell him that I may need him on a very dangerous and special mission that we have to keep in secret. If he accept it, there is no turning back. We will be only three at the moment; your man, Nikolay and me. I need you in the embassy, watching movements of the ambassador. Any help I need, I will ask you through Lieutenant Kosher. No one else has to know what we do. In addition, I would like to have a personal interview with your lieutenant. If possible, today.

- I'm sorry. Today, he is not at the embassy. He has finished his service and has gone. I will let him know tomorrow as soon he arrives. Would you like anything else?

- Yes, from tomorrow, the lieutenant must be off from duty. He will not step on the embassy, if it is not necessary. Grant him a special permit. I don't mind what kind of apology. Tell him, I'll be waiting for him tomorrow at the cafeteria Sputnik at eleven in the morning. He must be dressed in sportswear and a gray cap. From then on, he will be under my orders.

The Sputnik cafeteria was located in a small square behind the cathedral. Although he had never entered, he passed in front when visited the cathedral. It would be a good place, to interview Lieutenant Kosher.

- One more thing, I need you to give me the name and phone number of the taxi driver, Nikolay Ivanov and the number of the lieutenant. I want to speak to them personally.

- The telephone number, for special services, is 223.989.007. Tell him you are on Ken's side.

Kenneth, informed Jack of the way Nikolay worked. He used to frequently change the license plate of his vehicle for false ones, to perform certain jobs. His car was old, black, but neat. It´s similar to the vast majority of cars, which circulated daily in the city. Like many others, by its appearance, it went completely unnoticed.

JOSUÉ KOSHER, LIEUTENANT

Monday. That morning, it was raining heavily. It was eleven o'clock in the morning. Jack Brown, had summoned the young lieutenant Josué Kosher in the Sputnik cafeteria.

The morning had dawned quite gray from the rain. Jack Brown wore a white wig and mustache. He protected his head with a pet. He hid their eyes behind dark glasses. He could look freely anywhere and go unnoticed.

Jack was having a leisurely breakfast, sitting at the back of the cafeteria, reading a local newspaper. By going in disguise; he would avoid being recognized by the Belarusian secret police. He wanted to be sure that they were not following him. He did not want to put in danger to Josué, his new partner.

It was about to give eleven o´clock. A tall, slender boy with the appearance of a student entered decisively in the cafeteria without looking anyone. He wore sunglasses and a gray cap. He sat down at one of the tables. A waitress approached him to take note of the command. It was a slender young girl in her mid-twenties, blonde with blue eyes. She was really fine and beautiful. Josué was amazed to see her.

Jack noticed the face with Josué was looking at her. It was a real poem, what was happening to him. Jack couldn't avoid smiling. They could become a good couple, in the future.

For now, he would test him. He would watch him. He wanted to know how much he would hold out and behave during the wait. It would make him to wait a long time, before introducing himself.

Josué had a brief conversation with the waitress. They looked into each other's eyes and smiled, both complacent. Jack realized that he spoke and handle perfectly in Russian, just as Kenneth told him.

The waitress soon served him the breakfast. A slight smile intersected. Josué turned to look at her as she walked away.

While pouring the sugar into the coffee, Josué took the opportunity to look around him to the people who were inside the cafeteria. Distractely looked the time on his wristwatch. After half an hour has passed. Mr. Brown had not yet shown up. Apparently, he was not very punctual. Thought Josué would have to wait. He had no other choice.

Almost an hour had passed without contact. Josué absentmindedly checked the time again. He thought that some mishap could have happened to him. However, as long as he did not receive a counterorder, he would continue to wait for him in the cafeteria, it was agreed.

Jack decides to end the wait. He pays his drink and as he passes by, he hits the chair, in which Josué is sitting. He apologizes and leaves the cafeteria.

The waitress, who was watching the young man, notices that the old man has hit the chair in which the attractive young man was sitting.

She approches the old man, to ask him if there have been any damage when hitting himself. He replies that is fine, that nothing has happened to him and continues on his way to the cafeteria exit.

This replied her that he was fine, that nothing had happened to him, and continues on his way to the exit of the cafeteria.

Then, she would advantage of the incident to approach the young and attractive client, to ask him the same question, but what she wanted was to see him again. She felt attracted to the pleasant-looking young man, to offer him some other drink.

- No thanks. For now. I don't want anything else. -- Josué answers, thanking her for the service with a masculine smile. - I will pay you the breakfast. I promise you I will return another day, to take that drink. I hope to find you then.

When he is going to take the ticket, to pay for the drink, there was a folded piece of paper in it. He picked it up, while he paid breakfast. He puts a five-ruble note on the saucer. Wait for the change. When he was alone, had the opportunity to read the note, which stated briefly: "See you in an hour, at the Art Museum of the Republic of Belarus. Please do not be late."

He put it in one of his pockets. The old man who inadvertently stumbled in passing had left the note or, better said, he did so willingly.

His chief, Kenneth Diaz had adviced him about the behaviour of the special agent, Jack Brown, acted. He remembered that when he entered the in cafeteria, an old man occupied the table at the back.

During the time he was waiting for him in the cafeteria, he was already inside, watching him for an hour, without being noticed.

-ooOoo-

An hour later, they met at the Belarus Museum. The old man was sitting looking at the painting of the Proclamation of the Republic. Josué sat next to him.

- How do you like this painting, Mr. Kosher? -- He said pointing to the painting with his stick. – Which of the exhibited paintings would you like to have?

- My favorite paintings are the classic ones. That of the great Renaissance Masters. The rest respectz, but they are not to my liking.

- Okay, let's go back to what brought us here. I suppose that your boss, Kenneth Díaz will have put you in the background that one of our compatriots have kidnapped in this country. The situation is very serious and difficult, both politica and human. This matter must treated with the utmost discretion. I want to warn you that no one of our compatriots, from our government will help us. We will be alone. Whether we fail or not, our government will never recognize this service, and everything will remain as if nothing had happened. They will be silent. The case will archive forever. Both countries will not issue any communication on this matter. As if nothing had happened. They are not interested in it coming out. Our relationships would be broken.

- Is it possible to know, who is the person, who we have to find? – Josué questions. -- This is a politician or one of our agents.

Jack Brown, remain silent for a few seconds. He stares at him. He had no choice but to tell him the truth.

- The person we have to find is Phillip C. Harrelson. – He surprised when he heard the surname Harrelson. -- I suppose that you know he is the ambassadors´s father. He disappeared at this airport, moments before boarding for our country. He appears on the airline's boarding list, but he did not board the plane. We are certain that he has kidnapped by the Belarusian secret police. They are blackmailing the Ambassador. Aslong as they have the father, they'll not stop blackmailing him. The day they don't need him, they will possibly kill him. We have to act quickly, we don't have time. The time is finishing. They follow me and watch me closely

- I wonder, what does the diplomacy of our country do in this matter?

- They cannot do anything. For everybody, Mr. Harrelson got on the plane and left the country. This government is not willing to negotiate, because it would admit the kidnapping and carried out here in their country.

- So where do we start?

- Let's start by monitoring two policemen of the Belarusian secret service. They are two former agents of the former KGB. One of them is Inspector Igor Kustinov; the other is his hound, Gregorz Malenko. The latter known by the nickname "the butcher". They are very dangerous. We have to be very careful. At the slightest suspicion, they will not hesitate to make us disappear; to kill us. They have been following me since my arrival. They have been exchanging to mislead me, but have not succeeded. Fortunately, my instinct detects them right away like the plague. We will monitor them separately, I shall be the first, and you the second. You have to be very careful. If you see yourself in danger, disappears. Send me a message to my hotel. But if the situation is compromised and you have a difficult decision to make, don't hesitate to make it. Kill them! Our lives are the most important.

I recommend you change your clothes daily. -- He keeps talking to him. -- Next to the Smirnov cafeteria, there is a costume shop. It would be convenient if you bought a wig and a false beard, to change your appearance from time to time. From this moment, we will become their persecutors. Now we must separate. We will meet again around two oclock in the afternoon, at the hamburger joint on the main avenue. There, they usually meet at noon to eat. We will be at separate tables. When they arrive, I will signal you, to follow them.

Jack got up, leaving the museum, leaning on his cane. Josué, could not believe that the man he had been spoken, was Mr. Brown, who days before had been in his embassy office requesting permission to speak with his chief Kenneth Díaz.

He finished visiting the rest of the Museum rooms. He had enough time, until two in the afternoon, to meet with him. Apart from the museum's guards, it bearly had visitors, it could said that it was empty.

-oo0oo-

When Jack entered the Burger, Inspector Igor Kustinov and Gregorz Malenko were enjoying a double burger and French fries, accompanied by a mug of beer.

Jack asked for the exact same thing, as always. He tried not to eat any dish, not knowing how it was seasonedthat could make him feel bad and cause intestinal discomfort. He wanted to avoid at all costs, having to go through a hospital in this country.

Once served, he took the tray with trembling hands, the contents of which run the risk of falling to the floor at any moment, while he looked for a table to sit on. There were several free, but he chose to sit at the table next to the inspector and his bulldog.

They talked boasting of the use and power of wearing a badge. They commented of the terror, felt by some people, who were taken to the police station, to be interrogated.

They laughed loudly when they commented on how a boy had peed on his pants, when they beat him up, during an interrogation. The reason was none other that he hab the misfortune to collide with his motorcycle involuntarily, with a traffic police car. They accused him of attempted murder.

It seemed that everyone had agreed. Josué, too, was entering the hamburger joint. He stood directly in line at the checkout, like any customer, to orde from himr.

He appeared to be distracted. The only interest, that he showed, was to read the different types of menus, to have it chosen when he arrived at the checkout.

Once served, he looked for a table. He chose one that was free next to a window that faced directly onto the avenue. Before settling in his seat, he saw the indication that Jack gave him. Josué, appeared not to notice, but remained with the physiognomy of both individuals.

Josué was perfectly prepared, and trained. Like his boss, Jack. When he entered a place, he quickly captured everything that was inside, holding him in his mind. It was a habit acquired when he was a Mossad agent.

The police inspector and his friend, took their time for lunch. Apparently, they were in no rush to leave. Jack overheard them comment that two days ago they had lost sight of the new employee at the American embassy. That they had checked the flight boarding lists and the customs controls, in case he had left the country without them knowing about it, but he didn´t appear on any of the departure boarding lists.

Fifteen minutes later, they got up and left. Josué looked at Jack, but he made a movement to make him u derstand that he shouldn´t follow him. He montioned for him to come over to his table. Josué took the tray of food from him and sat next to Jack. No one paid him the slightest attention. The customers who were in the burger joint were normal customers, workers. They talking among themselves and they were only aware of them and their hamburgers.

- Those are the two men whom we have to watch. They've been talking about me; they haven't been able to locate me for two days. They are desperately looking for me. First, we have to investigate through another channel, to find out where they have kidnapped Mr. Harrelson's father.

Meanwhile, Josué finished his hamburger, Jack, separated to make a call.

-ooOoo-

Jack made a call to Nikolay. He was the third man of the group. He heard the noise of the telephone receiver picking up. But he did not answer the call. He was on hold, as if waiting for someone to speak to him.

- Hello, Nikolay. I'm calling from Ken. He gave me your phone, in case I needed your services. I'd appreciated you picking me up at the burger joint on the main avenue. My hip is killing me. I can't walk. I wait for you with my nephew.

He hung up the phone without saying a word. He knew he would come pick him up. A call from the American embassy, it was a very special service, highly paid and productive. Normally, he received the call from the embassy police chief, Kenneth Diaz. He gave his abbreviated name for security and as a previously agreed passaword.

It didn't take long for Nikolay to arrive. He had parked the vehicle outside the burger joint. Jack knew him from the airport arrival service.

Jack opened the car door to get in, but Nikolay indicated that it was busy. That it was request by other clients for their services, asking himm to find another taxi.

- Nikolay, I have called you, to request your services from Ken. This boy who accompanies me is my nephew. Start the car and let's get out of here.

- Well, where you want me to take you.

- For the moment, I need you to take us to a quiet place, where we can talk. I need you, beyond your car service. And for this, you look for a quiet place, where I can talk, without being disturbed.

- Very good. The place you are looking for is my garage. It is the safest place in the whole city. There we can talk without being disturbed. Also, I have a small fridge with some fresh beers, waiting for us, to drink while we talk.

- Great, take us there.

He put the taxi in gear, and began to drive away from the city center. He did not use the most direct route. He wandered mindlessly through the streets of the city.

Jack, let him be. He knew that Nikolay was doing a misguided tour. He kept checking in the rearview mirror if another vehicle followed him. When he was sure that he dosn´t followed, he left the city center, heading north to the Wolska Minska area. It was a calm looking area. Working people, honest but with low purchasing power.

He had the garage next to his house, but independent of the house. He stopped the taxi, getting off to open the entrance door. Once inside, he closed the metal sliding door, so as not to be disturbed.

The garage had of approximately forty square meters. It only had the front door. It lacked windows and interior ventilation. It had of a small workbench and a wall wooden board to hang the tools he used to fix his vehicle.

On top of the workbench, there were some broken parts. Due to the lack of existing spare parts in this country. They continue depending on Mother Russia, the spare parts for any vehicle. They had to get them on the black market, or they had to figure out how to arrange it.

In a corner, on the top of a roughly handmade bench by Nikolay, there was a small refrigerator, with several cans of beer inside. He took out three ones and handed them. They sat quietly to drink.

Josué and Nikolay remained silent. They were waiting for Jack, who calmly opened the beer can, and leisurely took small sips, keeping his gaze on the beer can.

- Nikolay, Chief Ken, informed that he has all your confidence, and that I can count on you for whatever I need. I would like to know, what is for you what I need.

- For what you need, the word says it all. You can trust on me and count on my services, for everything you need.

- Okey, Nikolay. First, I want you to give me a first service. This information is very important to me. However, I want to have your word that everything we spoke here it will remain here. It cannot go out this place. It is secret information and confidential.

- I give you my word. Tell me what it is about, and I will try to get it.

- A month ago, an American man of about sixty-five years, kidnapped at the same airport. This is Mr. Phillip P. Harrelson. The embassy cannot act nor do anything about. According to it, this person took the plane and left the country. This government is not going to help him, because if it did, it would recognize that they are the ones who kidnapped or held him retained against their will.

I want you to find out from your taxi colleagues if any of them have seen or heard anything at the airport. If possible the place where he can be held. -- Both listen to him in silence and he continues. -- As you will understand, this matter is extremely serious. I want to advice you that if they discover that you are snooping about this matter, you will be in serious danger. The truth is that you risky your life. This information will duly rewarded to you.

Any information or detail, no matter how small can be. Tell me! – He told him in a soft and authorization tone. -- This is to be among us. No one else. The embassador doesn't know what I'm doing. I don't want the embassy involved in a diplomatic conflict. Although, this government has caused it, they would not recognize it.

- There are, some taxi drivers, who work as confidants for the police. -- Says Nikolay. -- Some of them will surely know something. Many of my colleagues are barely relate to them. We know they're snitches and protected by the police. Many of my colleagues do not speak, because they fear for their safety.

- That would be very dangerous. You have to walk with lead feet. If they suspect the slightest, they could sneak around and we would all be in danger. Especially the kidnapped, who would soon get rid of him to cover his kidnapping, we have to be very cunning and cautious.

- Now, I remember! -- Says Nikolay – There's a fellow, who can help us. This is not confident, although he has a good relationship with one of them. I think they are brothers-in-law. I will see if I can get anything out of this matter.

- Remember Nikolay, maximum discretion. To stay in touch, when I call you, I will give you this password, I am Uncle Tom. If you are busy and you cannot answer me, so as not to compromise us, when you pick up the phone, answer with these words; Niko, speaking, I'm sorry you are wrong!

Josué remain completely silent. He didn't understand how he knew about the kidnapping of the ambassador's father. No one had news at the embassy. He remembered that on more than one occasion he had accompanied Mr. Harrelson when he was visiting the city.

His instincts told him that his new boss, the agent Jack Brown, was an experienced and highly qualified man; otherwise, they would not have sent him.

He had discovered in a few weeks what they did not know, despite security inspections of embassy staff, following established protocol.

They finished the beers, soon after, Nikolay left them in the city center. Separating himself later.

-ooOoo-

AN ILLIGAL ARREST

As soon as, Jack and Josué got off the taxi. Nikolay took a new passenger. It was an airport service. This race came to him, that not even dremed. Now, he would have the possibility to check if they were on duty at the airport, some of the confidant taxi drivers. He would try to get information, without raising suspicions.

Left the passenger, at the entrance gate of the airport, Nikolay parked in area he reserved for taxis.

Nikolay was reading a local paper. He saw the taxi, which was parking behind his; it was his friend Vladimir. He kept reading, pretending he had not seen him coming.

Vladimir got out of his taxi and approached the taxi of his friend Nikolay, who was still engaged in reading. He tapped on the glasswindow of the door where was sitting. Nikolay surprised. He got out of the taxi and they greeted each other effusively, as if they hadn't seen for centuries

- How about Nikolay, how are you? What happened to you? Come on. Tell me!

- Well you know how my old taxi is. I had a very serious breakdown, and I had to make a couple of pieces. I have ordered them, but they have not arrived yet. Can you imagine how long it takes? You know how this goes.

Suddenly several police cars appeared, along with another car following it, without a badge. This latter was a camouflaged car. The patrol consisted of six police officers in uniform and two plainclothes policemen, from the secret service.

Both wondered what would happen. It would have to be a big deal, when there more cops were going than usual and especially two from the secret service.

Nikolay stayed in the background. He recognized who were, the two plainclothes officers; one the inspector Igor Kustinov, and the other his inseparable lapdog, Gregorz Malenko, "The Butcher".

Some taxi drivers approached to curious what happenen. Soon after, they came out with an individual with his hands cuffed behind his back. They quickly put him in one of the local police cars, and they left the airport quickly, without wasting time, and with the sirens asking for clearing them up the way.

As soon as the police cars were lost of sight, the taxi drivers made a circle to comment on what had happened. However, in reality, they had neither seen nor heard anything. Just the sound of sirens and the creeching of the car brakes on arrival.

They were making cabals, trying to find out what had happened, when a smugly looking taxi driver came out from the airport, implying that he had seen and heard everything that had happened, in the passengers' VIP lounge. .

Being harassed by all his companions, and intrigued by curiosity to tell them, he took some time to become interesting and a little begging. He knew his was going to make the most of it.

He waited to tell it without saying nothing, until he was favored by the offer of some of his companions to invite him to a few beers.

He began explaining that the person who had been arrested and accused of being a spy. In his briefcase, according to the version of the customs police, he carried out documents and photos classified secrets, and a significant amount of money.

The taxi driver, named Mikhail boasted of knowing everything that happened inside the airport area. He considered himself an important man, because of the many contacts he had within the police. He was a petulant, easy-tongued guy when he got flattered. There was no need to push him too hard to make him valid, for his knowledge within the police.

- Apparently, it's not the first time this happened lately. -- He drops Nikolay, without giving it the slightest importance. -- There has been another time lately, a few months ago, as I understand it.

- About two or three months ago, more or less, another case similar to this occurred. -- Says Mikhail -- An individual of about sixty-five years, apparently of american nationality, was about to board, and they caught him, trying to get out secret documents.

- I would not like to be in the skin of these individuals, -- said Nikolay. -- Anyone knows, where they take them. Fortunately, we have a good police, considered one of the best in the East Europe. Our agents will take good care of them. Whoever does it must pay for it.

- Yes, yes. They will sing until polka, although they are not from here, nor do they speak our language. As you all know, one of the two policemen, among his companions is known by the name of the "butcher". Sure, the man will sing before gets to the police station, or, to "The Farm", which is considered the safest prison in the country. They assure that those who enter never come out alive.

- That name, it doesn't identife with the prison one. -- Comments Nikolay. -- It has the name of an educational center, for marginalized children.

- But as they say, there is another similar one, which is much worse than this one. Those who enter "The Nacional", I understand that, when they manage to get all the information out of them, are killed, incinerated and their ashes disappear by pouring them into the main drain of the prison, which waters go to the river.

- Poor american. I say this because of his age. That one lasts no more than a candy at the door of a school. Especially if the candy is given to my little nephew. -- Nikolay comments -- The bastard doesn't suck it, he swallows it.

Everyone laughs the occurrence of Nikolay.

- Well, the American is treated at a different way. Now, he is still alive and apparently in good health. You know, as long as they are interested, the police will treat him with "a lot of love" -- Mikhail comments, ending with a loud laugh. -- With much love! Yes.

- I wouldn´t like to be in either of the two prisons. –Nikolay comments. -- And less with the common prisoners.

- I think, he was held at some kind of farm in Borisov. At first they put him in the same prison, but political prisoners together with common prisoners, apart to be so many inmates crowded had to share cells. Which caused too many problems.

Political prisoners offered money to common prisoners to help them escape. What caused riots, fights and escapes of some political prisoners. Since then, to avoid these problems inside the jails, were separated and the politicians were taken to

"Farm II" in Borisov. The one that is heavily guarded. The american held there.

- Attention, comrades. -- Nikolay said. -- Passengers are coming out, let's go back to our cabs, we have got work. It was time. During the time I had my cab broken down, I needed to make money. I´m broke. Mikhail, we´ll see here tomorrow, I will be the first to pay you a mug beer. I don't like debts

Each one sat in their cab waiting for the passengers. To take them back to town

-oo0oo-

FINTAN'S SLUM

The phone rang repeatedly. Nikolay Ivanov cursed the phone a thousand of times and the one who was calling him. It was seven-thirty in the morning, and he had gone to bed late that night. At the insistence, picked up the phone reluctantly.

- I'm Uncle Tom. -- He heard a voice, coming thru. -- I need to meet you today at nine, at the entrance of the National Library. Next to the bus stop, I will be there with my nephew. Bye.

Nikolay quickly shaved with his electric razor and got into the shower. The cold water cleared him completely. He had just enough time to make breakfast, go out and to be on the spot at the time requested.

He did not know the name of the disguished agent. However, he did know that he liked punctuality. They arrived in unison, Nikolay with his taxi and Josué walking. The latter was leaving his beard grows. He had a closed black beard. In a matter of days he would have it quite grown, changing him the physiognomy.

- Gentlemen, where do you want I take you? -- Nikolay asked when they were in the taxi. -- Somewhere in particular?

- Yeah. Take us somewhere else, where we can have breakfast and talk quietly.

- Okay. Chief.

He put the taxi in movement to the north. They reached a suburb, outside the limits of the city. Most of their houses needed a hand of painting and good repair. Possibly, inside would not be in better condition. Their inhabitants belonged to the poor working class, and the most of them without work.

Some streets, the asphalt shone through its absence. There were only traces of what formaly a paved road. Potholes and drowsy abounded. The taxi seemed that was going to be unsquat, just like the ones inside.

Nikolay stopped the taxi at the door of a bar, which more closely resembled Ali Babá's cave. It was a real slum. Inside smelled of tobacco and cheap and bad vodca. As far as it fits, it was decently clean. His furniture was outdated, worn and poor. The inside was a copy of its outside.

It was breakfast time. The slum or bar, to name it somehow, was completely overcrowded, mostly jobless people, whose appearances chilled.

Many of those present were bearded, disheveled and dirty.

As soon as they entered, many of those in the slum greeted Nikolay, some even showing him appreciation. Jack Brown wasn´t surprised, that he was well known and showed him respect. While they greeted him, some looked between curious and surprised their companions. An old man, who could barely walk, used a cane, accompanied by a young boy.

Nikolay made his way between greetings and hugs, until he reached the counter, to greet Fintan. He was the owner of the slum, of Czech origin. His parent's emigrated while was a child. He orphaned being a child. He lived and learned on the street. Like most of those who lived in that suburb.

All those individuals formed the ghetto of the "residues of diverse communities and nationalities". Despite this, there was a great coexistence and good harmony between them. There was hardly any disturbance. They obeyed the owner of the bar.

They survived thanks to him. They shared everything, even a lack of work and hunger.

- Hello Nikolay. How long! What brings you here?

- First to greet you. I'm sorry I couldn't come sooner to have a few beers with you. But, a breakdown in my taxi has left me out of circulation, much longer than desired. I have brought some friends, with whom I want to have a calm and friendly chat, without being disturbed, while we´re-having breakfast. Do you have a place available right now?

- For you and your friends, I always have one. Follow me!

Fintan leds them through a door to the back to a small warehouse, which served him, at the same time as an office. He returns to the counter to make them breakfast.

When Fintan left them alone, Jack asked Nikolay, if he had obtained any information, to take him to the trace where the ambassador's father was hold.

Nikolay gave them an antecedent of everything that the taxi driver told them the day before. Jack and Josué listened attentively. Nikolay detailed them with the same words told by Mikhail. It was not difficult for both Jack and Josué to conclude that the ambassador's father was a prisoner in "The Farm II".

Fintan, the waiter, before go in, knocked on the door, entering with a tray on which he carried a hearty breakfast.

There was a moment during breakfast, which was silent. Nikolay and Josué looked expectantly at the boss, who was concentrating on his thoughts, tapping the table with the fingers of his right hand. They watched him without bothering him. A few minutes later, he stopped pounding the table with his fingers, breaking the silence.

- Well, like you, I have no doubt that Mr. Harrelson held in "The Farm II" prison in Borisov. We'll have to go to check it out. But, if possible, I would like to have first a map of the building. To know its distribution would give us an important advantage. We'd come by surprise, eliminating a percentage of the danger. Otherwise, we would forced to enter blindly, which would entail a loss of vital time, for the location and extraction of the prisoner.

We have less and less time. -- Keep talking. -- Time passes, too fast against us. I need you to try to get Mikhail out as much as he knows about the prisoner. Ask him if he knows the interior of "The Farm II", but without raising suspicions. Invite him and the other fellows to as many beers as they want, it doesn't matter, get everyone drunk if necessary. Let the questions asked by others, so as not to raise suspicions. If everyone asks, you are at less risk of being noticed. Also, I would like to know how this taxi driver gets the reports. Perhaps it will lead us to positive conclusions.

- Well boss. But for this I need to "refuel gasoline", the tank is almost dry. -- Jack, understand the hint and take from his pocket a wad of bills. He separates some bills and extend them to him. - Take a thousand rubles, for expenses.

Nikolay looked surprised. He did not expect such a quick and splendid reaction from the boss. Then he did the samething with Josué. This thanks him with a gesture, nodding his head. Although he had hardly had any expenses, he was using them from his own pocket, and he did not have much disponibility. His salary sent almost everything to his parents. With what he was left with, scarcely had to cover his expenses.

- Boss, can I intervene? -- Josué breaks into the conversation for the first time. Jack gestured inviting him to speak. - If the farm has remodeled inside, naturally, it will be very difficult to get a map. The only possibility would be to contact someone who had worked on it.

- Nikolay, take care of that matter. Try not to raise suspicions. And another thing, from this moment, we will be in contact through these mobile phones. -- He took two mobile phones out of his pocket. One handed to Nikolay, and the other to Josué. -- They are connected and programmed together with my mobile so that when one of us make a call, this call will go directly to the other two. In case of danger, we will save a call and time. Okey?

- Josué, I need you to carry binoculars in your backpack tomorrow, and a double-edged hunting knife with its sheath. If you don't have them, ask chief Kenneth. Tell him I need them. Do not provide any information, even if requested. Tell him that we are moving forward, although slowly, that we still don't know anything, and that we are encountering with many difficulties. Perhaps in a few days, I will call him and update him on what we have.

Josué paid for the breakfasts, leaving included a good tip.

They left the suburb. Nikolay dropped them in the city center, in different places. They agreed to meet the next day at eight in the morning. Jack asked Nikolay to come with the tank full of fuel.

This time, the last to get out of the taxi was Josué. He hardly spoke. He limited himself to observing and paying attention to what his boss said. Each time, he felt more comfortable working beside him, in the investigation. He admired how he was disguised. Really, he talked, walked and moved, like an old man. He knew how to treat and handle cold situations with great security and without flinching. But when he spoke, he knew how to make himself heard, and call the attention of those next to him.

When he left the taxi, Josué recalled that when entered the Fintan slum in the morning. The place, at firrst caused to him a very bad impression. As if they had led into a trap. He recalled that the first thing he did intuitively was to be on alert, to control any unforeseen. However, his boss Jack did not flinch, remained impassive, although he was sure, that he, too, had taken charge of the situation.

-oo0oo-

THE POLICE CAR

Josué put his hand in one of his pockets, stumbling inside with the thousand rubles his boss had given him for expenses. At one point, Jack handed out two thousand rubles without blinking. To Nikolay for drinks, and me for my expenses.

Jack had in his pocket a small fortune that more than one of that slum would have killed him if they would know what he had in his pocket.

Josué thought to go directly to the apartment; he shared with another colleague from the embassy. Despite the hearty and good breakfast, which he had a couple of hours ago, now wanted to have a good jug of cold beer, at the service's expense. Without realizing, he entered the Smirnov cafeteria.

He was not surprised, when he found Jack inside, sitting savoring a jug of beer. Josué sat at another table on the other side of the cafeteria. Jack made him an indication. He turned his gaze, following the direction of his boss, and saw that at a nearby table, Inspector Igor Kustinov and his lapdog, Gregorz Malenko, were talking in a low voice, but in animated chatter.

Jack Brown took the greatest interest in trying to listen the conversation that both had or part of the same. But the noise made by customers in the cafeteria was impossible to hear anything.

He was in no rush to have his beer. He would remain in the cafeteria, as long as necessary, watching the two policemen. However, apparently they weren't in a hurry to leave either. They ordered another jug of beer.

Jack had no projected any plan for that afternoon. Once, he finished drinking his jug of beer, he would order another one, accompanied by a combined dish, with his coffee and apple pie for dessert. Later, he would go to rest at the hotel.

They still stayed, almost two more hours in the cafeteria. Jack came out a few minutes earlier than the two police officers did. He waited for them to come out, watching them through the shop windows, located at ten meters away.

As soon as they left, a black car with driver picked them up. He had no doubt that the vehicle was one of the camouflaged police cars that used to go unnoticed, when performing special services. He stayed mentally with the license plate number of the car.

While waiting for Josué to come out, Jack made a call to the embassy security chief. Jack was talking to him for a few minutes.

- Obey my order. It is vital for the mission. You must have it ready from tomorrow. I don't know if I will need it. Don't tell anything the ambassador. Nobody else has to know about this matter. The walls ear. I hope you don't forget it.

Josué left the cafeteria. He was several meters away, waiting for his new boss to finish speaking.

- Josué, the inspectors, have gone in a black car with the license plate BK-805-SPD. Try to get through the embassy, to know what for what kind of services are used.

- Okay. Chief. Tomorrow I tell you something.

When he entered the hotel room. As usual, checked his personal effects. They had inspected it again. They never looked tired.

I hope one day they'll realize they didn't find anything. I'm not as stupid as they think. He thought.

He showered and got into bed. He needed to rest, to be fresh and clear of mind, for what was coming.

-ooOoo-

BORISOV

The day dawned rainy. Jack Brown had breakfast in the hotel cafeteria. He carried a plastic bag. After breakfast, he entered in the cafeteria toilets. He disguised himself as an old man. Then he walked out the back door facing the side street.

He walked up a stretch of about two hundred meters, to get away from the hotel. He stopped a taxi, which took him to Nation Square, about ten minutes before eight in the morning.

When he got off the taxi. On one of the benches in the square, Josué was sitting, who did not want to arrive late for the appointment. He used to obey strictly the orders received. Nor did Nikolay wait with his taxi.

Without greeting each other, they both slipped into the back seats of the taxi. Nikolay started without asking the address. Twenty minutes, it took to go out of the town. He made his way northwest of the city, heading for Borisov.

Inside the taxi, only was heard, the noise of the engine. No one spoke, nor uttered a word. They expected the boss to break the silence.

It would not take long for the silence to break.

- Ok Nikolay. have you got any information from your colleague, the airport taxi driver?

- Yes sir. We got drunk. Apparently, he has a brother-in-law, who is a policeman working at the central police station. All the most important matters pass through this police station, those related to politicians, spies, frauds and people opposed to the current regime.

The father of the American ambassador, Mr. Harrelson, is in "The Farm 2" prison. They also took there, that one they caught at the airport the other day. This is a Belgian diplomat. -- Nikolay go on. -- As for getting a map of the prison, if any, they are well kept. No one has a map of the prison. The only ones, who could give us information about the inside of the building, would be any of the workers who reformed it. Although, he told me, they were not local workers, because they didn't want the local workers knew how the inside the compound was. It will be difficult to find someone.

- Well, it doesn't matter. We will succeed, there is always someone, who knows something and is willing to cooperate. It does not worry me. Everything will go on.

- And you, Josué, do you bring what I ordered?

- Yes Boss. -- And immediately opens his backpack extracting from it, two knives used by the Special Forces. - One for you, and the other for me. -- I am familiar and know how to use it without cutting myself. – He said with a smile. -- Also, I bring you the binocular.

Jack took the knife out of the sheath. Watched it carefully. It was brand new. It was a deadly weapon and terribly silent, if you knew how to handle it with the required skill.

- I think, there is still a question pending to answer. - He asks Josué. - ¿Do you have any information, regarding the car?

- Yes, boss, I have it. The car with the license plate BK-805-SPD, is used in very special services. They have another series of vehicles, the ones that most of the population know because they are normaly used. Due to the number plate, this vehicle grants it, access to a series of official buildings and agencies, without the people in the car having to identify themselves. By itself, the license plate of the car is identifying.

- ¿Do you mean that if you arrive at any building, where there is a police control with a barrier, you are allowed to enter without prior verification?

- Effectively. In our records, we only have proof that there are four vehicles. They normally use them, to transport political prisoners, foreign agents or high figures, to whom they do not wish to publicize. If the people or the citizens do not know anything, the logical is that they do not ask questions nor try to find out.

Silence reigned again in the taxi. Everyone was pending of the road. It was in perfect condition. The landscape was full of beautiful contrasts. The car rolled through green meadows, as suddenly, disappeared and entered the mountains, from which could see one of the two rivers, which flowed placidly, crossing the capital. Borisov.

Nikolay wanted to break the silence. As a taxi driver, used to gossiping with his clients, during races or journeys that he carried out inside or outside the city. In the silence that prevails in the taxi.

- Boss, if you allow me, I will tell you about my country. It is full of history. Right there in the distance, as you can see, the Berezina River glides calmly across the plain. Most of its waters come from the snows that during the winter cover the summits of the mountains, which rise up in the distance.

Actually, Borisov's name comes from the Russian language. Its pronunciation is very similar, its true name in Belarusian, is written; Borysau. This city belongs to the Minsk province.

Founded in the year 1102, under the reigned of the prince Boris Vseslavich.

Belarusians, we are proud of our ancestors. Our history books report that in 1812, we inflicted one of the greatest defeats on Napoleon Bonaparte's army. This took place in the Battle of Berézima, during the withdrawal of French troops, after its invasion of Russia.

In the year 1871, the railway station built.

November 1917, our country became part of the Soviet Union. During World War I, we occupied first by Germany from the year 1,918 to 1,920, and later by Poland.

Later, unfortunately during World War II, Nazi Germany occupied us. The occupation lasted from July 1941 until July 1, 1944. During the time that the occupation lasted, a large part of the city destroyed.

There is a part of our history, which we often overlook, hide. We are ashamed to tell it. Around this city, the Nazis built six death camps. According to the data, which our archives have, that 33,000 people were there, exterminated.

Fortunately, after the war, our rulers made it a very important industrial area. Countless factories built.

Face with so many misfortunes and ruins, they had the people raised and given jobs, to remove the hunger. Among the remaining companies, and the most important in Borisov, two should be highlighted; the plant of electrical equipment for automobiles and agricultural machinery for tractors.

- It seems fantastic to me, that the city has recovered -- Josué commented -- But you has told us, that the Nazis built six death camps. What can you tell us about them? Do they still exist?

- No, I think was destroyed. -- Nikolay answers. -- Although, unfortunately a small piece of that horrible story remains.

- What do you mean; there is still a piece of that damnstory? -- Josué asks him, in a tone full of rage. He was of Jewish origin. -- Why, has it not disappeared? I don't think it's a place to be remembered or visited!

Nikolay stayed quiet. Prefered not to answer him. In the short time since he had known him, had never noticed him so irritated and upset.

They were reaching the city of Borisov. Nikolay knew it perfectly, its streets and squares. He went into the city center. When they reached the Old Square, all the parking lots were occupied. He waited for a moment, trying to find if there was a parking man. No one appeared anywhere.

The taxi stopped for a few minutes. Shortly after, a car left one of the parking lots, which was in front of the cafetería The Square. Moment that took advantage to park.

They entered the cafeteria, to have a snack. They sat at a table, which had not been empty for a long time. Previously, the used services were still on the table. They had not removed. The table located next to a large window, showed not only a large part of the Old Square, but also, a part of the imposing building that stood on the other side; the magnificent Cathedral of the Resurrection. Both, square and cathedral, built in the 19th century.

- What do you think! Do you like it? The truth. It's not magnificent! -- Nikolay says proudly, looking fascinated, both in the square, and in the catedral. -- Borisov, by itself, is an exceptional city. It is one of the few cities in the world, which has two cathedrals. The Cathedral of the Resurrection, the one we are seeing right now, and the Cathedral of Borisov, which takes its name from the city. Also from the 19th century

- Sorry, Nikolay. - Jack cuts him. -- We have not come to sightseeing. As soon as we finish our aperitif will leave. We can ot lose more time. We have to take a look at our objective.

- Boss, leave me a few minutes, I would like to finish with the Borisov´s history. I think it is important, and be connected to this work.

- Go ahead, Nikolay, I hope you don't take too long. The time you have is until we finish our apperitive.

- Thanks boss. I said that they built six death camps and that they subsequently disappeared. That is true, but there is a small part of one still remains. The part I refers to, is the offices of the officer. This part of the pavilion rebuilt and turned into, "The Farm 2".

When the story ended. A bitter grimace of pain appears on Josué´s face. As a Jew he was, he would never forget the pain caused by the great massacre that led to the extermination, for those of his race. Most of their ancestors were exterminated in different concentration camps of other countries. It had been a long time since all the Jews had accepted it, but was not why they had forgotten it and it was less painful for them.

His parents had kept alive in his memory the family's story, so that they would not forget it, but without feeding his hatred nor anger. God, wrote the history of Israel, and of its people centuries before. His father told them, it was God's designs.

From then on, they resigned accepting it, without wondering. Why?

- Thanks for your history class, but it's time to get going. -- Jack says, getting up with difficulty and with a slow and tired step. -- Come on. We have wasted a lot of time!

Josué pay the bill to the waiter. He leaves him a ruble tip. He thanks him. At that moment, the waitress from the Smirnov cafeteria came to his mind. He wouldn't mind seeing her again. He wouldn´t mind seeing her again. He would stop by on his return, to greet her and take her drink pending.

-ooOoo-

THE PRISION. "THE FARM 2"

Nikolay put the taxi on the way to "The Farm 2". He had never been there, but he knew the way. He had informed of how to get there. He wanted to show Jack that he could trust on him. Although, he had not spoken or stipulated the price for these services, he considered that it was not the time to discuss it. He trusted the boss fully. He knew he would rewarded. So far, had given him more money than he could consume in beer for a long time.

He tried to remember his face the day he picked him up from the airport, to take him to the embassy. But when he tried to compare it to his characterization now, it would be difficult for him to remember.

It wasn't take long before they reach the road. "The Farm 2", was located at a distance of five kilometers from the town. There were no buildings or houses around it. The compound was rectangular built on one level. It wasn't very big. It could pass through a farm, if not because, in each of its four corners, they had built a watchtower. Its walls were five meters high. At the top of its walls, they had installed a strong electrified fence, which made it difficult to enter and exit the building.

Inside, apart from the entrance control in an annex had the bedrooms for the guards with the shower services. Apart from the prison commander's offices. In the rest of the building would be the dungeons, where the prisoners would locked up.

They didn´t find a place to park, it was also prohibited. Josué took several photos of the building as they passed by. Along the road, a large electrified fence surrounded the prison. Some posters warned of the surveillance cameras on the outside of the compound, warning that anyone who tresspassed through their established security zone without authorization run the risk of being arrested or shot, not asking in case of resistance.

As they passed the road in front of the building, Jack made use of binoculars. Quickly, he got everything needed. From the two front watchtowers, he saw how one of the guards in the right watchtower was using his binoculars, too. They guards controlled all movements that occurred outside the building. Surveillance was total.

- Nikolay, is there any chance of going back to Borisov, but by another road. I do not want to cause suspicion if they realize that it is the same vehicle. When we have passed, I have verified that from each of the surveillance towers, they have been following us with their binoculars. I do not think they could have seen the car license plate, but we cannot take the risk that they will recognize the vehicle.

- No problem, boss. I have changed the license plate. The one it carries belongs to the car of a friend of mine, who died in an accident and his car burned. This happened a long time ago. He also had no family. They will not be able to locate us. But the best thing is not to raise suspicions.

Later on the road, there was a detour indicating the entrance to the village on the north side. They took it, but upon entering the city, on the opposite side of the arrival, they had to move around the streets with the car, until they reached Borisov Square. They parked next to the second cathedral, which gave the name of the city.

They entered the Café Berezima. The air inside smelled of stale tobacco and vodka, like Fintan's. Its furniture seemed to have never renovated since its opening. Jack realized why Nikolay had stopped there. They ordered three beers. There were not as many customers, as in the "The Old" cafeteria, located in the very center of the city.

Although, Jack had an idea of what the interior of the prison could be like, but it could also be very wrong. He would try to get any information, however little it was.

As he sipped his beer, he looked around and saw that all the customers of the bar were elderly. Possibly retired.

At a table, an old man was looking with some sadness and unease at a glass of vodka, which turning in his hands. The glass was empty!

Not to mention a word. He got up and sat down next to the old man, knocking the beer jug down on the table. Josué and Nikolay remained attentive to his movements. Something was up.

- Many times, the life treats us ungratefully. We give it everything and in return, we receive nothing. We can hardly have a miserable glass of vodka or beer. May a compatriot invite you to a drink? -- The old man stares at him, surprised and intrigued. It had a long time since anyone had invited him for a drink. Also, by a stranger. -- If I bother you, I'm leaving.

- I have no problem sharing your company, if a good double glass of vodca and a chat accompanies it. -- The old man replied. -- Excuse me sir, I do not know you. Are you from Borisov?

- Yes sir, I am your fellow citizen. My name is Yuri Sokolov. I left from here many, many years ago, being a child. It is a long time that I wished to have come. I wanted to see my city before God takes me with him, to the other side. I have found the town changed. On the north side, a few kilometers from here, I have seen a military camp. It is completely fenced around it. With threatening posters that are scary.

Jack asked the waiter for another double glass of vodka, for his fellow. The old man remained silent until the double glass of vodka brought to him.

- That is a high security prison. Only for high-ranking politicians and military. It´s said that those who enter do not usually leave alive. Not long ago they entered two new ones, almost in a row. Politicians as they say.

Most of the guards live here. -- Continues. -- Although they do not usually relate to the people of the town. But there is a guard, who comes from time to time, precisely to this bar. His felows have to take him out, completely drunk. Sometimes his tongue looses when he is completely drunk. That´s we know that.

- And how long has that prison built? I suppose the town's people built it. To give them work.

- No. Most brought them from other towns. Many of those who worked, we have not seen them again. I don't know what happened to them. -- He was thoughtful for a moment. -- Now I remember, I met a young man, who was working on the construction of that compound. He told me, as they had built the inside, the side behind the wall. This boy said they built twelve individual cells, around the central courtyard, equipped with doors and bars of such thickness that it would be impossible to damage them with a bomb. A guard corps with eight cots for each of the guards, the room of the officer in charge of the prison. And, the four watchtowers.

- Uufff. Its story produces chills. The chief of the prison, I suppose he will live inside the prison.

- Not, that it goes? This man lives in the city center, in a small dead end street, behind the Old Square. His house is the only one with a garage. There is a plaque, which prohibits to park on the street. Everyone knows him is afraid to confront him. He does not relate to anyone here. He goes in uniform and armed. He boasts of his position and likes to strut. He comes from time to time, so that, he remember who is in charge here. Even Borisov's police chief is afraid of him. He knows that he feel hated and feared by the people of this town. But that gives him more satisfaction, and makes him feel stronger and more authoritative.

- Well my dear friend, I must leave you. -- Standing up. Jack gave himself a small massage on his right leg, at the same time he leaned on his cane. Before leaving, he asked the waitress to serve him another double glass of vodca. He paid the amount of the drinks. -- Thank you for your kind and interesting talk, friend.

- Thanks for the two glasses of vodca, buddy. -- Jack Brown was heading towards the door.

- Come on guys, let's go back.

Josué asked the waiter the bill for the drinks. Then, Nikolay and Josué followed Jack.

- Anything new, boss? -- Josué asked him, inside the taxi. -- Was it worth it, your talk with your friend the old man?

- Yes, much better than I expected. This morning, I planned the possibility of how to enter "The Farm 2". Now, I have a much better knowledge and easier to enter. With this second option will give us more and better possibilities. Let me think. We will take action as quickly as possible.

They made their way back in silence. They knew that the assault on the prison would be from one moment to another. Josué looked at his boss out of the corner of his eye. He was lying in the back seat next to him. He was with his eyes closed, as if asleep. Imbued in his own thoughts.

He took advantage of his boss, who was absorbed, to pay close attention to his characterization. Sometimes when he got out of the car, he intended to help him to get out. Although sometimes, appeared to be asleep. Josué was sure that his mind was always working and thinking about how to enter the prison. He left nothing to chance.

It was not long before reaching Minsk when Jack sat up from his seat.

- Nikolay. I need two trustworthy young men. They must be experienced men in combat, military trained fighters. That they are not afraid of anything, and that for a handful of money, they don´t mind risking everything on a single card. They should preferably be single. Without a wife and without children. I don't want to leave widows or orphans behind me if I can avoid it.

They soon reachen the center of Minsk. Before getting out of the car, he says to Nikolay.

- We need weapons, also. If you know who can provide us, I want you to take us right now. I will personally choose them. I will check if are in good conditiones, before buying them. We will wear black clothes and balaklavas, and gloves of the same color. You pick us up tomorrow at The Nation Square, at nine in the morning.

They both got out of Nikolay's car before reaching the square. They entered a hamburger. Jack took the opportunity to inform Josué, during dinner, what the old man had told him in Borisov's bar.

After dinner, they went their own way.

-oo0oo-

<u>NEW MEETIN WITH FINTAN</u>

Ten minutes to nine in the morning. Josué was sitting on one of the benches in the Nation Square, awaiting the arrival of Jack and Nikolay.

Like every day, that weather invited to do so, a good number of people gathered in the square, especially the elderly and retired. Most gathered to play chess, to talk about football, and others to comment on their memories or to read the newspaper with the news of the day,

It was about to strike nine. Jack hadn't made an appearance in the square. Josué looked at the time on his wristwatch. The time coincided with the clock sound in the square. He was surprised not to see him.

Because of his Jewish origin, Josué instructed by the Mosad had acquired the necessary temperance to know how to control the nerves and have patience. Normally, he was not disturbed or concerned, for no apparent reason. But he was a little excited inside. He had not been involved in an important and dangerous mission for a long time. He felt that it would take place much sooner than he had imagined.

Last night, at dinner, his boss had told him how they would carry out the assault on the prison, to free Mr. Harrelson. Perhaps, there would be a part, which he would not have told him. Although he was sure that, he had everything planned and controlled beforehand.

He was concentrating on his thoughts, when he heard the horn of a car near him. He turned and next to him, Nikolay's taxi stoped. He was about to open the door to enter, when someone passed him.

- Sorry sir, this taxi is reserved. -- Josué told him. -- You will have to take another one.

- Don't worry; it will serve both of us. -- The tone of the voice was familiar to Josué. -- Starts Nikolay!

Josué was surprised again. The man sitting next to him, in the back of the car did not look at anything from the previous day. He was dressed in a shirt and cowboy suit. He wore sports shoes, a wig and a red mustache. He also wore glasses with round lenses. He looked more like an intellectual teacher.

- Boss, I was worried, I thought something might have happened you. I did not see you, and you were sitting quietly next to me.

- I know. I saw you look at the clock several times, but you don't have to worry. If you remember correctly, we agreed that in the event of any unforeseen event, a phone call would put us on advice, and contact everyone.

- Sorry boss, it will not happen again.

- I don't like you to apologize. I hope you don't do it again. The insecurity causes difficult and contradictory situations. In our work, we cannot afford it. Insecurity can provoke in an instant, to go from life to death.

Josué went to answer him, but preferred to remain silent. He was about to apologize again. He would consider it for the future.

Nikolay, while driving, couldn't stop staring at him in the rearview mirror, the characterization of the boss.

- I see you are taking us to your friend Fintan's bar. He asks Nikolay. -- Is it true or am I wrong?

- Yes boss. Everything is prepared as you ordered.

- Well, when we get there you introduce me, like Robert Brent. As I suppose he will remember Josué, you introduce him like Tom O´Brien; I will take care of the rest.

When they reached the suburb, he parked the taxi at the back of Fintan's bar. Nikolay hadn't had time to stop the taxi's engine when the person watching through peephole behind the back door opened it swiftly to meet Nikolay. They get out of the taxi and go in quickly.

- Hi brother. -- Says Fintan to Nikolay. -- I have everything ready. ¿Can you tell me what these gentlemen need so urgent?

Jack got straight to the matter. Each passing day, there was less time to get Mr. Harrelson's father out of prison. Any oversight from within the embassy would be fatal.

- We need five pistols with silencer. Five bulletproof vests. Also, two extra chargers for each one. The weapons must be clean, and without serial numbers, so that they cannot identified. However, we´ll destroy them, when we finish our work.

- Very well, follow me! -- He introduced them to a room attached to the warehouse. It was the place where Fintan had served breakfast two days before. Inside there was a true arsenal. -- You can choose the ones you like. They all work and are in perfect conditions to use.

Jack checked carefully, the arsenal there were on the shelves. He was highly interested by the Taringas guns, which he carefully reviewed. He considered them to be in good condition. He set them aside and put them on the table. He chose five with their silencers. From a counter, took ten spare chargers. Two for each gun.

- Tom, do you prefer these ones on the table or any one from the shelf? -- The question referred to Josué. -- Or do you prefer a machinegun?

 - No boss. You have chosen the best. I have already used them before, and it seems to me, that will be very useful to us.

- All right then, let's go to the price. Friend Fintan, I know perfectly well the prices at which the gun market moves. I ask you to give me an affordable price, so as not to have to haggle or have to get out of here without them. Although, I know business is there to make money, but without abusing.

Fintan stares at him challenging. What, did this red-haired guy think he was to give to him? Jack holds his gaze. Fintan gaze was hard and firm. Jack knew what making deals with a guy like Fintan wouldn't be a problem.as lon as he stood firm. When the came to an agreement, they kept it. His word was law. Everyone respected him

There was a slight lapse. They studied each other. Neither of them showed the slightest sign of weakness. Fintan was tall and strong as a rock. Jack would not like to engage in hand-to-hand combat. Like most of the slum, dwellers were men hardened in a thousand battles. They lived from what at every moment presented itself.

Josué and Nikolay remained silent, watching how they challenged each other with their gazes. They both thought the same. It would be a very close match. They would not take part in it.

- The material, which you are looking up, is difficult to get in the black market and you know it. I understand that you know about weapons, as much as I do. So I'm not going to deceive you. If you are interested in weapons and vests, their price is twelve thousand rubles.

- Okay, but I need a bag to take them with me.

Josué stepped forward and grabbed a sports bag off the shelf. Introduced weapons and bulletproof vests. Meanwhile, Jack took out a bundle of bills from his pocket. He paid Fintan the price agreed. Twelve thousand rubles.

They left the room where Fintan had the armory. Jack ordered some beers for everyone. Fintan returned to the moment with a tray of beers and dry nuts. He entered accompanied by two young men, between thirty-five to forty years of age.

-ooOoo-

KRICHENKO´S BROTHERS

- Here you have some beers. Invite the house. -- Fintan said, leaving the tray on the table. -- I introduce you Alexander and Markus Krichenko. I hope you reach to an agreement. I leave you alone so that you can speak calmly.

Alexander and Markus remained impassive, without uttering a word, standing up in the middle of the warehouse. They did not flinch when they saw that watched closely by those in the warehouse. The redhead with intellectual glasses struck them, above all. Jack liked the presence of the two young men. They were athletic and looked fit. The brothers had a great resemblance.

- First of all, I should like to know, if you had performed military service, let's call it out of the ordinary, dangerous, in the army. I mean, if you had been in combat. The job I need you for, is extremely dangerous, we will run a great risk. I want you to know that we´ll face dangerous people.

- Sir. -- Answer Alexander. -- My brother Markus and I have been fighting in the city of Mostar, in Bosnia-Herzegovina. During the time the war lasted, unfortunately, we have seen everything, the good and the bad of a war. For us, a war is as bad as having no job nor money to take away our family's hunger. If the work is for a good cause, you can despose of us. We will assume the risk.

Jack liked the sincerity, which Alexander answered. The two brothers, due to current circumstances, desperately needed money, to help their parents and their family. He knew they would do anything for money.

He had no choice but to trust them. He had less and less time left to free the ambassador's father.

- I want to make it clear enough to you that this is difficult and risky matter. It´s a question of taking out, a person, from a maximum security prison, who has been unjustly imprisoned. He didn´t brake the law in this country. They use him to blackmail and extort money from their family. If you accept, I want to make it clear that you have to follow my instructions. I will not allow any sign of doubt or weakness in this mission. If everything goes as planned, the operation will execute in a few hours. If any setback arise, for the sake of the group, and the person we are going to rescue, I will change the planning inmediately. I do not admit that my orders discussed.

- My brother and I agree. We need the money. Our debts press us in charge; above all, we need to pay the debts that our parents have contracted so that they do not take away their house. We´ll not allow seeing our parents the street, which would kill them. For this and a thousand more reasons, which are irrelevant. We accept it with all the consequences. If you do not mind. How much will the service report to us?

I´ll pay you for the service one hundred and fifty thousand rubles. I hope this figure be enough to pay all your pearents debts and live comfortably for a time. I will pay you when the service performed. Whether its goes well or f it goes wrong. Once it has started.

The brothers looked at each other, without believing it, one hundred and fifty thousand rubles, it was more than they could imagine. They had never earned so much money, nor thought he would pay them an amount like that. All debts would removed and they would have to live for a time. They would even open a gym, the dream of their lives.

- Yes sir, we accept. Tell us what to do.

- I remember. Don't have any doub that the work is dangerous. It'll be fine, if you obey my orders without hesitating. I want to make it clear that we will try to do everything possible to avoid deaths. If you follow my instructions, it may not be necessary to get to that point. But, if circumstances force us, you have to act without hesitation. Before they have to fall than we. -- He says them in a soft but authoritative tone, which admited no doubt. -- From this moment, you have to be ready to act. I do not think it is necessary for me to tell you this is a secret mission of the utmost confidentiality. I want you to know that, we will be alone on this matter, and nobody will help us. If they catch us, we will not receive any kind of support. -- He pauses, to check if there is the slightest sign of doubt. But everyone stands firm. -- You will receive instructions through Nikolay. From this moment on, you have to be available.

 By the moment, he had already given enough information to the brothers. They got the message, leaving the warehouse and the back door of the bar.

Josué checked for his boss's countenance that he had liked the two brothers. However, he was still silent and with his mind was somewhere else. As he was always up to something new.

- Nikolay. We will not use your car for this service. We need one with more capacity, such as a van. What are the chances of getting a van with capacity for about eight people? If you need to buy it, you change the color of the paint, and you put fake plates on it. After the service, we get rid of of it, so don't leave any clues.

- So suddenly, it's difficult. I know some people who have a van, but we cannot trust on them. The only possibility is to use our friend Fintan's van. He want to get rid of it. It´s for a long time he wants to sell it. Some seats can attached and it can serve us.

- As long as the engine runs perfectly. It'll be a matter of giving him a hand of black paint, and changing his license plates. Nikolay, tell Fintan to come in. I'll talk to him.

Fintan didn't beg. It took him a few minutes to get back to the warehouse. Drying his hands with the white cloth used by the waiters. Afterwards, he placed it on his shoulder.

- Here I am for what you like to order.

- Fintan, I need you to provide us with a van with eight seats. If you are interested, you tell me the amount for two days rent and the price if I had to get rid of it, so as not to give clues or compromise anyone. Preferably, in black color.

- Boss, if you are interested you can have mine. I put it eight seats, the ones I have in that corner. -- He points to a corner at the end of the warehouse. – I paint it black, I change the license plate and the front trims, I do it everything you asks me. The price is three thousand rubles. Double if you destroys it. As you will see, it is all about money.

Jack accepted the deal. He needed the van. Fintan took advantage of the moment and the circumstance, because Jack needed his help.

Fintan had a curious and special character, he gathered all the qualities; gangster, arms smuggler. He would sell his mother for a handful of rubles, if necessary. For money, he would do anything.

Jack accepted the deal. He needed the van. Fintan took advantage of the time and circumstances, but Jack needed his help. He was a curious and very careful character, gathering the qualities of; mobster and arms smuggler. He would sell his mother for a handful of rubles, if necessary. For money, I'd do anything.

- Okay, I want it ready for this afternoon at last time. Nikolay will pick it up. Now, I'm paying you fifty percent of the rent. -- He took out from his pocket a bundle of bills of one hundred rubles. -- When I return you the van, I will pay you the rest or double, according to the service.

They signed the agreement with a handshake. Fintan took the moment to squeeze his hand and try to calibrate Robert the redhead's strengh. But it was found that his opponent returned the squeeze blunty and in the same way with a smile. Fintan was convinced that he had in front of him a tough and dangerous adversary, despite his appearance.

- Well, gentlemen, I bring you some beers. -- Fintan says. -- I'll be back in a moment.

Meanwhile, Jack gave Nikolay the last instructions, before he left.

-ooOoo-

COMMAND TO BORISOV

It was half past four in the morning. Jack and Josué got into the van. Inside, the brothers, Alexander and Markus, were sitting in the back.

Fintan had done a good job. The van painted in black, and the seats placed. Now its capacity was greater than what he asked for. Ten seats. The tank was full of diesel.

As they left the city inmediately. Once on the road, Josué took out of a large bag; five black jumpsuits, five balaklava and five pairs of black gloves. Everyone change their clothes, except Nikolay, who was driving. He would do it later.

- The balaklavas and the gloves we will put them on, before doing the work, when we reach our destination, for now it is not necessary. Put it on the shoulder strap. Thanks.

As the van continued to devour kilometers on the way to Borisov. Inside, only the monotonous noise of the van's engine could heard. Jack was sitting in the front, next to Nikolay. They unknown the last instructions. They would receive them at the right time. No one asked any questions.

Jack had left it clear. The less they knew, lower risk would have the operation failing.

- Gentlemen, we have about two hours to go. You can have a rest until we reach our destination. Before we will make a brief stop in Borisov. We will stay awake, making him company along the way to our friend Nikolay.

They obeyed him. They sat as well as possible in the seats of the van. Rest was going to be difficult, but they would try to do it. There was a few kilometers to get there.

An hour and a half later, the lights of the city could see at the distance. The van would take about twenty minutes, to reach Borisov.

When they reached the Old Square, Jack instructed Nikolay to park the van on the street, which had no exit. It was located at the back of the cathedral.

- Boss, the parking prohibited on that street. See the plaques placed on each side of the street. If we park here, will be fined, apart from not letting any car pass and will block the street. As you see, this street is too narrow. The van will not be able to leave any car from the garaje nor enter.

- Don't worry, Nikolay. If someone comes out or comes in, I will personally apologize. Besides, as long as we parked on this street, the van cannot see it, which gives us some advantage and will pass unnoticed. Don't you think? Have a rest. I will make the first guard. But change your clothes. Like everyone else, I need you fresh and rested, by the time comes.

One last thing. -- He tells them. -- When the garage door opens, you should put on your balaklavas and gloves, and be aware of what happens. It is clear!

- Yes Boss. - They answered in unison - Nikolay, you will lean on the steering wheel and don´t move, whatever happens, as long as I don´t order you. It´s understood.

- Yes Boss. Whatever you order. We´ll not move.

He pulled the seat lever. He put it in the best position, to lie down and give himself as comfortable a head as possible. He had not rested during the night. He had been driving it.

-oo0oo-

COMMANDER DiIMITRI VASILIEV

It was seven thirty in the morning. The door of the garage begins to open. Jack wake everyone up and ask them to remain silent and stay tuned.

- Please, remain silent and lying in your seats, so that he does not see you. Put your balaklavas on. Nikolay lay on steering wheel and don't move! As if you were still asleep. I´ll take care of him. Attention everyone, it´ll be a matter of a moment!

The prison chief almost collided his car against the van. He didn´d expecte that a van parked on the street. Just a few meters from the exit of the garage. There was a plaque indicating its prohibition. The van left no room to go out. It occupied the whole street.

He rang the horn repeatedly, but the driver of the van did not flinch. Surely, he was drunk as a vat. If not, he wouldn't have dared to park on his street. He was mad. How had it occurred to him to take a sleep and rest on his street? The horn of his car rang repeatedly with rage. The driver was still unaware

He couldn't believe it! He considered it as a challenge to his and authority. Or, he was too stupid, mad or he did not know him, otherwise he would not have dared to park never on his street.

He rung the horn again, repeatedly. But the driver of the van was still lying on the steering wheel asleep. Seeing he didn't move, he opted to get out of his car, heading for the van. The driver was going to find out who was, Dimitri Vasiliev, chief of the prison "The Farm 2". The driver didn't know whom he was. As he approached the van, he drew the club from his belt. He was going to give him a lesson!

Jack was sitting in the other front seat, next to Nikolay's. Watching Dimitri Vasiliev approached the van in a threatening way. Jack warned Nikolay not to move, and the others stay watching over. They had to act quickly. Surprise was essential to the success of the mission. The chief approched the van, hitting with the club furiously, the driver's-side front door, denting it.

- Sir, sir, please stop! -- Jack says to him as he was getting out. -- Please don't keep hitting the van, our boss is going to kill us when sees it dented.

- Damn you, the one who is going to kill you, is going to be me. -- But the commander the prison, "The Farm 2", was surprised by the speed with the driver's fellow replied, who stopped the blow, disarming him and leaving him immobilized and unconscious, without realizing what had happened to him.

Everything had happened so fast, there were no witnesses. On a lonely street, where there were no cars parked, for being forbidden.

But if any neighbors who lived there, if they had seen what had happened, would never say anything. They would be glad of what happened. Everyone hated him and were afraid of the Commander Dimitri Vasiliev.

They put him in the van. After a few minutes, he began to regain consciousness. When he realized what happened, was naked. His uniform had removed and he was lying on the floor of the van. He tried to move. But, just stayed in the attemp. He was gagged hands and feet tied. The three guys in the van were dressed in black, wearing gloves and their heads covered in balaklavas. Two of them watched him closely, without taking their eyes off him.

In front of the van was another vehicle. Although he couldn't see it, because was lying in the van´s floor. The noise of the car's engine was very familiar to him. He knew it perfectly well. It was his car.

When he really regain consciousness, the chief Dimitri Vasiliev realized that a perfet-trained command had kidnapped him. Dressed in black, with balaklavas, gloves and bulletproof vests. Belt with semi-automatic pistols with silencer.

Jack removed him the gag. He did not wait, to threaten them.

- I hope you know what you are doing. The kidnapping of a government agent is punished by death. So the best thing you can do is let me go, and I promise you I will not retaliate or take action against you. Believe me, untie me, damn you, before I repent and break my promise!

Silence was the response the abductee received. Jack gaged again, unanswered or paying attention to his threats.

-ooOoo-

ASSAULT AND LIBERATION. "THE FARM 2"

About fifteen minutes passed, when suddenly the van stopped. It was heard the sound of a metal door opening. Immediately, the van begins to move slowly, and stops again after a short drive. There is the sound of the door closing, and then the sound of another security door opening.

The two guards on duty at the gate control stand up to salute their chief Dimitri Vasiliev, the car passes in front of them. He returns the salute. The car stopped in the parking lot, once the van was inside the prison compound.

From the back of the van, the brothers jump surprising the two guards at the entrance. They urge them to remain silent. They were disarmed into the guardroom, gagged, and stripped of their uniforms.

Meanwhile, Nikolay takes the opportunity to park the van, next to the car´s chief, Dimitri Vasiliev.

Jack and Josué geo into the guard corps. There they meet four more guards; they were passing time playing cards. They surprised by the presence of the two intruders. They tried to react, but had no time. The two individuals were dressed in black, went heavily armed and ready to use their weapons. They stripped them of their uniforms, gagged and immobilized them. They couldn't believe what was happening. The prison considered high security. They never thought that would assaulted.

Josué took in charge to leave the prison incommunicated with the outside world. Except the cameras that kept surveillance around the building. He placed Nikolay on surveillance for the camera outsides, to avoid any unpleasant surprises. Like the one they had just done.

They laid the guards down on the cots, tying them so that they could not move. Jack instructed Josué and the two brothers to bring Chief Vasiliev out of the van.

Dimitri Vasiliev considered himself a good observer. He was awaiting any failure or false movement on the part of the assailants, which could lead him, later, to their identification, to capture them and make them pay with their lives for their audacity. But, if they ran away, it would be a stain on his file that he would have to live with for the rest of his days.

Jack ordered his commandos to change their jumpsuits for the uniforms of the guards, without taking off their balaklavas. They changed into an adjoining room, out of the guards' sights, and their chief. He wanted to avoid the risk of being identified by means of a defect, brand or birthmark.

Two of them took the place in the guard post. From the outside, everything seemed normal in and out of the prison compound.

To can controlled the compound, they had to take prisioners the two surveillance guards in the watchtowers at the front of the building. Josué and Nikolay took care of them. In half an hour, they took over the prison compound. Now, they had to free the prisoner.

Meanwhile, Alexander and Markus were watching the prisoners. Nikolay remained in the entrance checkpoint.

- If some try anything, kill him! -- Jack says to those who were guarding the prisoners. His intention was to intimidate them.

Not to do it. -- Also, don't let them speak. Although gagged it is difficult.

Jack, accompanied by Josué, took from the guard corps, the keys of the cells where the prisoners were locked up. When reached the hallway, they came up with a surprise.

At the background in front of a window, the guards of the back wachtowers were playing chess.

They were so involved in the game; they did not turn to find out who were the guards who had just entered. What a surprise they were going to take! They could not suspect that were two intruders. The prison had been designed to give maximum security, intruder-proof.

- It was time for our relief. -- Says one of the players. -- Is breakfast ready? We are hungry!

- Breakfast, we'll give it to you now. -- Jack answers. -- I don't think it'll do yoy any good.

They are surprised by the answer and by the voice, but much more when they turn and find two men in front of them, in their uniforms, covered in a balaklava. After the moments of surprise, they knocked over the table and tried to get their weapons. They didn't give them time. They encountered the cannons of two semi-automatic pistols before their eyes.

They disarm them, take off their uniforms, and immobilize them by locking them in one of the empty cells.

Only three cells were occupied, the rest were empty. The first one that opened was Mr. Harrelson's. He was lying on a cot, unaware of what was going on. He was in good health. He had no signs of violence nor having been tortured.

- Mr Harrelson, fear not! We have come to set you free. Do you know the people locked in the other cells?

- Yes, one of them is an English agent. The other is a Bulgarian diplomat. Both accused of espionage. They have done nothing. Like me.

- All right, let's take them. -- He said to Josué. -- Take them out of there, and let's leave as fast as we can. We are late. Please don't talk. Everyone must remain silent.

As soon as they got to the guard corps, Jack distroyed the central surveillance camera, and extracting the recording tape, burning it. They could not leave any visible trace of their passage through "The Farm 2.".

- Boss, what do we do with the prisoners? - Josué asks when they are alone - I kill them!

- No, we are not murderes. We will leave them immobilized. They will severely punishe when they found them naked and gagged, the prison assaulted, the prisioners released, and the guards naked and gagged. Possibly, they will be the next ones to occupy the prison cells. -- He pauses and continues. -- As soon as the central headquarters have no contact with them, they will come to check what has happened. I suppose that will come at the latest tomorrow, and they will be released. Then, they will have to give many explanations, and we will be far away and out of their reach.

Before leaving the prison, Jack commands all vehicles parked inside the compound be disabled. Also, the electronic opening system of the fence, and of the doors inside the prison encosure. To exit will use the manual system.

Once the work is done, they settle into the van. Nikolay sets in motion and minutes later, they lose sight of the distance, the rectangular building of the damn maximum-security prison, called "Farm 2".

-oo0oo-

THE ESCAPE. Three for one

When they came to the main road, Jack ordered the balaklavas removed. The prisoners looked at their liberators with admiration.

It was a commando perfectly prepared. Its components were young. The elder was the redhead who was the chief. Since their release, none of them had opened their mouths to say a word. They just obeyed.

- Gentlemen, I´m going to talk to you very clearly and I want to know that I´m solely responsible for your freedom. -- He addresses the free people. -- I mean I have no actcd under any flag and have no received an order from any government. If they catch us, as I said before, nobody will move a finger for us. Now my commitment is to take you out of the country and make you disappear.

- Sir, we will be eternally grateful to you for what you have done. -- Mr. Harrelson tells him. -- We will never forget it.

- Gentlemen, it is still early for the thanks. Before, we have to leave this country. Until we don´t get out, our lives are in danger. Now more than ever. We have assaulted one of the safest and most important prisons. We have free three of the most important prisoners, for this country, and they will do their best to find us. If they caught us, they´d kill us without mercy.

Silence comes back inside the van again. Jack, stay quiet and thoughtful. No one dares to bother him. Those who know him know that, as always, he is up to something.

- Nick. I want you to take us to a safe place, where we can accommodated these gentlemen. Just for one night. I can't risk taking them to the embassy. The police following the orders of our friends, Inspector Igor Kustinov and Gregorz Malenko, will heavily guard it. In addition, I have to treat personally some businesses, which I must leave resolved before leaving this country. -- Jack continues. -- It is very important for everyone that this matter ends well. I count on your trust.

- Boss, count on it. – Nikolay answers. It is the first time that someone responds - You always have our trust.

They were on the road for an hour and a half. In the distance could see the city of Minsk. Nikolay devited north of town. Before arriving, he turned into a secundary road, which had little traffic.

Minutes later, they crossed one of the many suburbs of the town. Then stopped the van at the door of a two-story house. Nikolay gave Jack the keys to his house,

Josué, before leaving the van, left the bag in the van with the clothes used in the assault on the prison, with the order to burn it. They got out of the van, quickly going into Nikolay's house. No one had noticed his arrival. The street was empty.

Meanwhile, Nikolay locked the van in the garage, taking out the taxi and leaving it in front of his door. In the garage, he got rid of the clothes, gloves and balaklavas burning them along with the bag.

When he returned, the guests housed, upstairs. There were two bedrooms, one with a double bed and the other with two beds. A bathroom with a shower plate and the toilet.

Upon Nikolay's return, Jack asked the guests to come down and gathered in the living room. Jack was taking a photo to each one with the camera he had found on the sideboard in the living room.

- Gentlemen, we have to stay here until tomorrow. From this moment on, we all have to remain as quiet as possible. As nobody were in the house. The lights will go on and off, according to Nikolay's custom. This is his house and we have to act, according to his custom, so as not to call attention, from the outside. We must do everything possible, to go completely unnoticed, or, we will put ourselves in a dangerous situation, as well as, to our dear Nick.

Jack takes Josué by the arm. He separates him from the group to inform him.

- I have to go out with Nick. -- He said him. -- While we are away, I want you to take care of the surveillance, along with the brothers. Distribute the guard as you consider convinient. You must have your weapons ready at hand. Do not hesitate to do what is necessary to keep these men alive. You know this have been our mission.

-ooOoo-

NEW DOCUMENTS

Nikolay and Jack left the house. They went to the garaje and took out the taxi parked at the garaje door.

- Boss, where are we going? -- Nikolay asks.

- I need to do several assignments this afternoon. First, take me where I can get passports for our guests. This is very urgent. I want them by this afternoon. Second, we have to find suitable clothes for our guests and for me too, and third, we have to bring them supplies.

Nikolay started his taxi on the way to the suburb on the other side of town. He parked in the back of Fintan's bar. The horn sounded three times. Immediately the door oponed and passed inside. Fintan receives them.

- How about friends, how did everything go?

- So far good, friend Fintan. I still need your help, so I have to do business with you again. I hope you treat me like a good friend and customer and don't bleed me.

- Depends on what you ask me. If it is in my hand, do not doubt that I will serve it you at a good price.

They looked at each other and both smiled. Fintan was a ruffian in the broadest of the word. However, he kept his code of honor, fulfilling what promised, under the agreements of the power of money. They were getting to know each other, much better than it seemed at first glance.

- I want you to provide me with four passports of different nationalities. I need them for tonight. The photos are in this camera. You must give me a price for them.

- Boss, what you are asking me is very difficult to get and so suddenly, it seems impossible to me. There is hardly any time for anything.

- Friend Fintan, let's forguet ceremony. I know those tricks, don't work with me. Give me the damn price!

Fintan gave a loud laugh. It was the first time that the boss had lost his nerve. He had altered.

- Let me a few minutes to make a call. I'll be right back.

They sat down while waited for his return. It didn't take more that ten minutes. He came in smiling and bragging about getting anything he set out to do. He wanted to show the boss his power.

- Good. Everything arranged. It took me a while to convince him, but I did it. You will have your passports in the late this afternoon. The price is twenty thousand rubles. Believe me I have tried to get a better price. But the passports will be as if had used. Nobody will note the difference. They will go with entry and exit stamps from different countries, even with the entry visa in Belarus.

- Fintan, you are a truhan and a damn bastard. You take advantage because you really know I need them. I hope this will keep secret. I mean your contacts.

- Don´t be afraid, friend. We´re all running at great risk. If they catch us, they'll shoot us all, in less than twenty-four hours, the first one to me. They are behind me for a long time, but I am still free.

- Okay now, we will settle account. I'll give you back the van, with some dents in the door on the right. Nikolay will bring it to you tomorrow. If you are interested in weapons and bulletproof vests, I will return them to you they have not used. You can resell them again. You will not associate with them. Tell me your final price!

- I see that you are a good negotiator, if you are the same for everything; you have to be very good at your job. I will put you a good price, I want to have you as a client. I hope you recommend me to your friends.

- You don't have any doubts. Be sure I am! Ask Nikolay. I'm the best, but please for our health don't test me. -- He answers Fintan. -- It's best to remain like good friends. Personally, you are more useful to me in this way. -- Jack pauses and go on. -- You know you're making a lot of money on this matter, without no risk.

Fintan spends a few moments thinking, reconsidering Jack's proposal.

- My offer is this. You give me back the van, the weapons and the vests. I take the care of removing the damage to the door and painting it in its previous color, my price now is thirty thousand rubles, passports included.

- Done! -- They both shake hands. The deal closed. -- Tonight when I come to collect the passports, I will pay you as agreed. Tomorrow, if possible or the day after tomorrow, Nikolay, will return you the van and everything else.

- Okay. Boss, you command.

-ooOoo-

After this visit, Nikolay took him to a warehouse to buy clothes for the liberated. They could not go through the border and to pass the customs control in the clothing they now wore. They were woefully dressed.

- Boss. The police will probably guard the mall. If you like, I'll take you to a warehouse, where you can buy everything you need. They're friends and they will charge us a good price, we're not in danger and they won't ask questions.

- All right, let's go before closing.

They took thirty minutes to reach to warehouse. They entered with the car inside the store. The owner greeted Nikolay. Everyone knew him. He had many contacts.

- Hello Gustav! Let me introduce you to a good friend of mine. He wants to buy four suits, four shirts, ties and shoes.

- How long without seeing you, Niko. I already missed you. What about your life. -- Gustav replies. -- Follow me; at the back, I have the suits and the accessories.

Jack looked up in the shelves where the shirts were, picked up four discreetly colored shirts from the hangers. Then went where the suits were hanging.

Before choosing them, he made a call. Nikolay instinctively tried to pick up his phone. Jack motioned for him to ignore the call. Then remembered that any call, was connected.

- Yes boss, no news. Everything is still quite. How can I help you?

- Ask our guests about the sizes and shoe numbers they wear. I'm waiting online.

The answer wasn´t kept wait.

- I tell you, boss! In the suits, two of them wear size fifty-two and Mr. H. fifty-four. For shoes, one uses forty-one, and the other two use one more number.

He chose a suit for Mr. Harrelson. For the other two jackets, complementing the color of the trousers with that ones of the jackets. The black shoes according to the sizes provided. For him, he chose pants and jacket, too.

It was beginning to get dark when they left the warehouse.

Jack Brown, make a call.

- Yes tell me. -- A voice answers on the other side. -- Chief Diaz speaking.

- I'm Jack. Do you have the package ready for me?

- Yes sir, everything is ready. Tell me what to do with it.

- In about twenty minutes, I will be there with Nikolay to pick it up. When arriving I will make a call for you to come out the back and deliver it to me.

- Okay. I will do so.

- Thank you.

-ooOoo-

They reached the back of the embassy. He hadn't given the taxi time to stop when Chief Kenneth Diaz left the embassy, handing him the package.

- Mr. Brown. What news from the ambassador's father? How's it going, do you need help?

- Everything is going well. Probably tomorrow, I will send you news with Josué, who will inform you carefully. Please do not comment anything, not even with the ambassador. Every time, we are closer to get our objetive. It is a matter of hours. Believe me!

They quickly left the rear of the embassy behind. Nikolay made several detours before reaching his home. He had to be sure they were not following him.

When they returned it was late. Just a light noticed from the outside, that it was on. It was the light from the living room on the ground floor.

When they entered, only the sound of a television heard. Nothing else! The guests showered and were upstairs in their rooms, resting quietly. The two brothers carried out the surveillance. On the ground floor, Josué was watching television, pistol in hand.

- Hi boss. No news.

- Hello Josué. Please upload these bags to our guests. They contain clothes and shoes. Let everyone choose their size, the suit is for Mr. Harrelson. They have to wear it tomorrow. The shoes have their numbers. The black bag is for me.

Before leaving the house, he left Josué in charge of the black bag. Apart from the clothes, which was inside, there was another bag containing the money. He took out thirty thousand rubles and put them in a commercial plastic bag.

He didn't take long to come down. Nikolay set out again for the Fintan slum. They had to collect the passports.

-ooOoo-

Fintan was waiting for him. As soon as they entered, he took out a used envelope from his desk drawer, which containing four passports in; French, English, Norwegian and Russian.

The passports gave the impression of having used with some frequency. They had entry and exit stamps from different countries. They documented with their entry visas and the exit documents prepared.

- Really good. -- Jack said him. -- Expensive, but very good. Friend Fintan, I have to admit that you too are good at your job. In this envelope contains the agreed amount. Count it!

- Boss I trust on you. I know everything is in here. --He said, while moving the envelope. -- No need to count it.

- The money is to count it, friend Fintan. I'd rather you count it, there may be a glitch.

At the insistence, Fintan counted the money. Everything was in order. The banknotes were used of different amounts and difficult to locate. This Robert thought of everything. He knew how to do it

- Everything okay, boss. I hope I can continue doing business with me.

- I have yet to ask you for another favor, but I am not going to pay for this one, you have left me dry, I do not have a penny. I need eight large steak sandwiches with fries potatoes and eight bottles of cold beers.

- That's done! In a few minutes, I will prepar them. In the meantime, I'll bring you a beer with some snacks. I hope you recommend me.

 - Possibly. I cannot say no. I have very important friends. I will recommend you. Nickolay will be in charge of contacting you.

-ooOoo-

They returned to Nikolay's house. On the way back Jack was thinking about how to get them out of the country. The liberation had complicated. But, now there are three people instead of one. He had no choice but to take them out from this country. If he had left them in prison, he had no doubt that they would have executed, to silence the kidnappings, and to partially exonerate the failure of the assault.

He had to prepare an escape plan, that night. They were all still in danger, as long as they didn't leave the country, and the longer he took to get them out, the harder it would be. The police would be looking for them all over the country. Removing heaven and earth.

As soon as Josué heard that a vehicle had just stopped at the door, through the peephole, verified that those who arrived were his boss and Nikolay. He hurried to open them the door. They all gathered in the dining room. Nikolay served each of them a sandwich and a beer. The fried potatoes placed on a dish on the table.

Nobody spoke. They were all hungry; they had not eaten anything during the day.

When the improvised dinner was over. Jack handed each of them their new passport.

The ambassador's father, Mr. Harrelson, could not contain himself any longer and hugged Jack sobbing. Francois Renau approached to thank Jack and the rest of the people, who had risked their lives to get them out of that damn prison.

When things calmed down, the calmest was the British agent, Richard Whitmore, who took the apportunity for a moment to approch Jack.

- I want to thank you for not leaving us in prison. I will be eternally grateful to you; I thought I would never see my wife and my two children again. If at any time, you need my help, I am at your disposal. At anytime and without condition.

- Thank you. Now, I prefer that you cooperate with my colleagues. -- He asked Nikolay for the gun, and handed to him. -- Help keeping guard of the house, taking care of the people upstairs.

- I'll be delighted, Jack.

Jack makes a sign to Nikolay. They left the house.

-oo0oo-

A VISIT NOT DESIRED

Once in the vehicle, he asked Nikolay to take him to the Hotel Markesal. He had to pick up his passport, which held at the reception desk and his backpack also, which was in his bedroom. Before arriving, he takes off his wig and his blond mustache. He changes his mustache, the one that appears in his passport.

 - I need to get back my passport, and if possible, also my belongings. I don't want my passport to fall into the hands of the police. I have my fingerprints on it, and I don't want them to be in their files. I don't care if they have a photocopy of the passport.

When they arrived at the hotel. Jack got off the taxi and went directly to the reception desk.

He asked the recepcionist for the key to his room. This hesitated; he had not seen him for a couple of days. He didn't expect him to show never more up. There was a moment that he did not know what to say, the key was in the locker. When the receptionist picked it up the key to hand it to him, his hand trembled visibly. He stared at the receptionist. He became more nervous. He did not know how to give the guest an explanation.

- Tell me! ¿Are waiting for me in the room? -- He asks. -- How many people are there? ¿Are two true, the Inspector Igor Kustinov and his fellow, Gregorz Malenko?

- Yes sir. But please, I can't tell you anything else. Among other things, I´m not only playing only my job, but something else. They can accused me of collaborator and I coukd have a hard time going to jail.

- Well, let's make it easier. -- He says, pulling out a large wad of bills from his pocket. -- I pay you for my stay, I don't ask for the bill, I give you a good tip and you give me back my passport. I don´t go up to my room, and you take my backpack and everything in it. If the police don't take it. When a couple of days pass, the housekeeper will inform you that the room has not occupied, and you file the complaint to the manager of the hotel. He will report me to the pólice and everyone happy, and we all win.

The receptionist, was thoughtful for a few seconds, the idea was not bad. He did not think twice. He reacted quickly. He took the passport out of the safebox, handing it to him. Quickly, he calculated the amount of the stay, at the highest price of the rooms.

Jack was aware of the account he was making. He knew he was taking advantage, but it was not the moment to waste time for a derisory amount, that it did not mean anything to him. He paid the amount and gave him fifty rubles as a tip, so that he would forget his passport.

- For your sake, if they ask you about me, remember that I have not been here. About my passport, you know nothing. Do you know what can happen to you if the police know that you deceived them?

- Thank Sir. I do not know anything concerning your passport. For any purposes since yesterday, I haven't seen you neither your passport.

Jack returned to the back of the hotel. It was completely night. The alley was poorly lighted. It hardly noticed that a vehicle was stopped. Because of its black color and the lack of light, it wasn´t possible to distinguish what type of car it was nor the license plate number. Likewise, it could not see it, if it was busy or not. The light on the hotel's service door, too, was off.

- Start it up slowly, without turning on the lights, until we get out of here. I don't want they see the license plate through my bedroom window and be able to locate you. -- Jack lay down in the back seat so as not to be seeing. -- I have two visitors in my room right now. My room window gives to this alley.

- Boss, will they they heard about the operation and be watching all the foreigners. How about your passport?

- Don't worry, the receptionist has returned it to me. He will keep his mouth closed. In exchange, I have paid for my stay without invoice. I have given him a good tip and he will keep my backpack and everything inside. I think it is a good deal.

-ooOoo-

When they got out of the alley, Nikolay looked in his rearview mirror, checking that his passenger was sitting in the back seat. He thought that the boss was a very inteligent person and a good negotiator. He had done a clean job, even in the movies couldn't do it better. Without flinching, and most importantly, without causing victims. No one would have dared to assault the safest prison in this country, "The Farm 2". Only him.

Nikolay thought, he had more than enough material to write a book. He would do it in the future. It would be a bestseller. It had all been so easy that he didn't know if it had been a reality or a dream. What a bundle the prison chief Dimitri Vasiliev, had to deal with. When they discovered them; bound, gagged, and naked.

Nikolay, while driving on, thought that all what happened in the assault on the prison would remain covered and secret, forever. They would not publish it. It was a big problem, shared equally between the Secret Service police and the government. A fact that would never published.

Before returning home, they left the car at the door of the garage.

They arrived late. Only the dim light from the living room TV was on. The rest of the house was in darkness. It didn't notice, no movement inside. The guests were resting in the rooms on the first floor.

Josué had distributed a guard service. Every three hours they would alternate in the relay. One upstairs and onother one on the **groundfloor**.

Although, Nikolay lived in a quiet neighborhood, he had fortified his house. He put bars on the windows and the front door armored. He lived alone. For his work, he spent most of his time outside. It endowed it with the maximum security.

Josué was waiting for them in the living room, watching television, when he heard the noise of the front door open. He stood up, carrying the pistol in his right hand, ready to use it. He wanted to avoid surprises.

- Hello boss, no news. The guests are resting. Agent Whitmore has agreed to collaborate. I've put him watching upstairs. I was waiting for you.

Nikolay went to the kitchen to make coffee. Meanwhile, Jack took the opportunity to update Josué about the individuals who were waiting for him in his room at the hotel. Both, without saying anything, assumed who the people were.

Nikolay entered the living room carrying a metal tray with a coffee pot, four cups and a sugar bowl. He placed it on the table and served each one a cup. The cup left was for the english agent, Whitmore, who joined the meeting.

The coffee was good. Nikolay had good taste. They took it without haste, savoring it slow and silently. Everyone was watching the boss, who, as always, he was deep in his own thoughts.

Jack was thinking about Nikolay. He noticed his manners and behavior. The least he had, it was a taxi driver. He was polite and an educated man. He knew the history of his country, without any doubt. He was aware of everything that was happening. Whatever asked to him, he got it.

Jack suddenly came back to reality. He began to speak in a low voice, like himself.

- I really don't know if the reason why they were waiting for me in the bedroom. Perhaps, they relate me to the assault on prison and the release of the prisoners, or perhaps because lately, I have become an invisible man for them. They have lost my tracks for several days and they have not seen me. -- Jack comments, staring at the cup of coffee. -- They have a contact at the embassy, but even inside the embassy, no one on the staff knows my mission, except Ken and Josué. I do not think that should be the reason, rather I incline that they have discovered the scape. But they lacked of clues to relate me to what happened

Suddenly, he remained silent. However, he continued staring at the contents of the coffee cup, as if he were a seer trying to see or find out inside, what was happening right now, and what would happen the next day.

- Josué, I want you to gather in the living room the brothers, here and now, except Mr. Harrelson and Mr. Francis Renau.

Nikolay returned to the kitchen to make more coffee. The night would be longer than expected. Jack gathered them together to give them the last news.

Moments later, they remained in absolute silence. Those gathered were waiting to receive news of what he had planned. They presumed that would give the last instructions.

- Gentlemen. -- He began to speak addressing those who were gathered. -- We are at the end, to conclude our mission. So far, everything has gone well, apparently. I say apparently, because everything seems to be calm, as if nothing had happened. But it's not like that, let's not deceive ourselves. I believe that they already know what happened in the prison. I have been at my hotel to get my luggage and my passport. At reception desk, hanging on the shelf, there was my key room. I noticed some nervousness from the receptionist, just when he saw me coming. His hand trembled when he extended the key to my room. I forced him to tell me what happened. He warned me that there was a couple of police officers waiting for me in my room. I retrieved my passport from the reception safebox and left my backpack with all my belongings at the hotel. If I had gone up to my room, I would have forced to kill them and put the operation in danger.

I guess they are moving heaven and earth, trying to find out the people that assaulted "The Farm 2". They are hitting blinds. -- He continued talking. -- But they do not know where to start looking for. Everything have executed cleanly and without a trace. Now we have to finish off the operation. Now comes the most difficult part. I have to get our guests out without any risk. I think to get them out of the country by plane or train, it is impossible. Naturally, everything will heavily watched. I think the best option; I mean the least dengerous from my point of view is taking the road to Vilnius. It is two hundred kilometers away, and if they stop us, we will move better to defend ourselves and to run away. If the situation becomes more difficult, we will not hesitate to act. Nikolay, give me your opinion!

- Well I agree with you, boss. The best option is the road to Lithuania. It is the country, where the border is closest to Minsk. Normally, it´s very busy, maybe that will help us to go unnoticed, although, I suppose it will be, heavily guarded. The border is usually open at eight in the morning. I have done many services. If when we get ther, they haven't found out about the prison, I don't think we´re in any trouble. Sometimes a good tip makes easier to get out.

 - How long will it take to reach the border?

- Approximately two hours. No, we're interested in going out earlier or too late. About nine o'clock in the morning it's a good time. We can find a lot of traffic on the road or, on the contrary, a relatively quiet day.

Normally, the people use to arrive a little later at the border. Sometimes, the border police officers delayed in opening.

- Well. We´ll go in two cars. In your taxi, Mr. Harrelson and I. In the other taxi, Josué, Mr. Renau and agent Whitmore. Behind the second car on a motorcycle, covering covering the two cars will go Alexander and Markus. You will go dressed in biker clothes. You'll keep a distance of about fifty yards with the second car. We'll all go armed. When we reach the border and gone through, you can return. Remembered the weapons, and bulletproof vests, must delivered to Nikolay. I have promised to return them. Is it clear? -- They all nodded. -

Jack continues speaking. -- Nikolay, I want you to call your friend now, I need him with the taxi at eight in the morning without fail. -- Then, addressing Alexander. -- ¿I suppose you know how to ride a motorcycle?

- Yes Boss. We know, and we have a motorcycle of great displacement. We will use it for this service if you need it.

- Very well! That avoids me not to rent one. -- Then addressing to Nikolay. – I want you to give me back the cell phone for Alexander tomorrow, so we can stay in touch on the way to Vilnius.

- Well, gentlemen, that´s all. Everybody get some rest. I need you first time in the morning, fresh and rested. Tomorrow, it´s going to be a hard day. Josué, I relieve you from surveillance, for three hours. Then you will replace me.

Seconds later, the house was silent and in complete darkness.

-ooOoo-

It was seven in the morning. The eight people gathered in the dining room. The only thing on the table was a coffee pot full of coffee and a plate of cookies. It was everything in the house for breakfast. They hadn´t bought food so as not to raise suspicions.

Jack called the Krichenco brothers. He took them to a separate place. He wanted to settle the debt incurred.

- Like, I promised you at our first meeting, this envelope contains the amount of one hundred and fifty thousand rubles promised. Now one of you has to bring the motorcycle. I suggest that whoever goes leave the money at home, in a safe place. I don't want you to carry it on this service. If something happens, you would have to give many explanations. As soon as you return, we will leave immediately.

- Boss, in half an hour I'll be back on the motorcycle. -- Alexander said when leaving. -- Bye.

Jack take advantage that Nikolay was in the kitchen making coffee. It was time, to hand him over the envelope with the liquidation for the services rendered.

- Nikolay, we have never spoken or reached an agreement for the extra services provided. As promised, I said I would pay you for the service, whether it did or not. In this envelope, you will find seventy-five thousand rubles. For the services done. I hope you collect the weapons and the bulletproof vests and return them to Fintan with the van. Now tell me, the amount that I have to pay your friend for the service of his taxi.

- Boss, I'll take charge of that. I will pay him. Let me tell you that you have my respect and consideration. I will miss you. It is long ago I'd had an affair like this. I have no doubt that you are a great person. The best, that's why they sent you. I will be at your service, as long as you need me. You have done a fine job. If one day this affair comes out to the public, they won't believe it. It has been a pleasure to be under your command.

- Thanks to you. Without your help, it would be impossible for me. Excuse me; I think I heard the noise of a motorcycle. Check if Alexander has arrived.

Josué was at the door. He was always vigilant. He was awaiting Alexander's arrival.

- One moment Josué. - This turns and Jack gives him an envelope. - For your expenses.

- Thanks boss. He takes the envelope and puts it in inside his vest pocket. Because of the thickness, he assumed it could contain about twenty thousand rubles.

When Alexander is at Jack's level, he tells him.

- Boss, everything okay. Fake plaque, full tank. For our part, we are ready to go.

- Well. As soon as the other car arrives, we'll leave.

Jack looked at his wristwatch. It was eight o'clock in the morning. A horn sounds. Nikolay's friend's car had just arrived.

- Gentlemen, good luck to everyone. The decisive moment has come to finish what we started. Remember that we have to finish the mission cleanly, as up to now, but if circumstances compel us, we must act without hesitation. In all the missions I have involved in, I have never had a lost a man. If action is to be finished with all the consequences. I want everyone to return home today safe and alive. -- Everyone was listening carefully, including the guests. -- Markus, I want one of you who doesn't drive takes this cell phone. Pressing this button becomes operative and the call received simultaneously on these two phones. They will used in an emergency. Also, before any doubt or something out of common. You have to communicate to me.

Jack makes the call and his Markus phone rings with Josué's.

- Okay. Boss, understood. -- Markus answers.

- So, everyone on movement. Good luck.

The first car starts, followed by Nikolay's. Behind them, the the Krichenco brothers followed the second cars in the motorcycle maintaining the distance.

They drove at a normal distance, maintaining the speed in the town. They left from the northwest, taking a detour that led them to the main highway, towards the border with Lithuania.

There was plenty of traffic, though it flowed regularly. In some sections the traffic ran placidly. Other times, when traffic converged with roads that joined the highway of nearby villages, caravans formed, making it impossible overtake. The orders were very clear. Do not draw attention, under any circumstances, and keep the distance. Everyone hab to be in eye contact.

Jack consulted Nikolay about the possibility of deviating down a secondary road, to avoid possible police controls. But, there was only one and they were in it; the highway. For now, traffic was running without major traffic jams. Everything was quiet.

After about seventy kilometers, there was a great retention. Josué reports the retention is due to a police check control, and asks for instructions.

- The instructions are; tranquility, move on, and be prepared for any eventuality. Getting out of the queue would attract their attention. We would discover ourselves. We must all remain alert, and ready to intervene, as a last option, if the occasion requires it.

There were two highway police patrols in a checkpoint inspecting vehicles, meticulously and without haste, one car after the other.

When the first car driven by Vladimir reaches the checkpoint, the police checked the documentation. They looked at him and let them pass. They were looking for an older man with white hair. None of those in the car had those characteristics. They passed control, without a hitch.

Between Vladimir and Nikolay's car, four vehicles separated them. When they were about to get the checkpoint, suddenly, something happens. The chief of police answered a call. When he hanged up, he ordered to withdraw from control, and they quickly went back to town.

- Boss, something big must have happened, suddenly they have left the surveillance control, and they have left. - Josué says, over the phone. -- For now, this will give us some respite.

For Jack, the news is a really a break. But despite having the road claer up, he was not willing to allow his men to relax. He took the phone, and transmitted maximum alert. It could be a false alarm, to make them fall into a trap.

- Gentlemen, pay attention with a little luck, in an hour we can finish this matter. Please, I ask everyone for maximum attention and concentration. We cannot be trusted. Surely, it will be a second checking at the border.

An hour later, they arrive at the Lithuania border. There was a lot of racking people and goods. Agent Whitmore and Mr. Renau were in the queue at the customs window, closely guarded by the custom police, to have their passports stamped, a requirement from departure from the country.

When it was their turn, the police requested their documents. Passports with visas, and checked their luggage. They returned their luggage. They wore in the bag; a sweater, shirts and underwear. They returned them the stamped passports with their departures authorized. They passed to the other side, without problems.

Jack had taken two weights off his shoulders. Now it was his turn with Mr. Harrelson, to whom they would surely be looking for, even under the stones. Despite the bad times spent in prison, he was quite firm and calm, showing no sign of nervousness. Which partly reassured Jack.

The customs police officer, who was checking Mr. Harrelson's documents, was inexperienced. He looked several times at the passport and at Mr. Harrelson. The latter reacted quickly when he realized that he was not wearing sunglasses in the passport photo. He took them off and with a smile, giving him to understand that he was the person in the photo. The young man stamped the passport, giving him the exit.

Next, it was Jack's turn. They checked the passport, issued in Kiev of Russian nationality, and by diplomatic profession. They sealed it immediately, without checking the contents of the bag.

Jack helped Mr. Harrelson move across the border. At the entrance to Lithuania. I knew perfectly well, how the custom officer and the police of these countries worked.

After the questions of rigour, which customs agents systemly ask foreigners entering their countries, they managed to enter Lithuania.

The border was about five kilometers from the nearest city. They took a taxi to go the town. Vilnius.

Jack asked the taxi driver to take them to the American Embassy or Consulate. He paid the taxi with Belarusian rubles. The driver accepted the money without discussion. The ruble quoted well and the tip was worth it. For the expense of changing a currency from one country to another.

At the entrance to the embassy police control, Jack identified as a special agent of the GSSS agency. He requested that the American Ambassador, Mr. Glenn Withdraw received them inmediately.

For about an hour and accompanied by the three men, he informed the ambassador of the mission entrusted. Although the most difficult has done, for Jack Brown, a mission is not finished, until it is finished!

Jack asked permission to the ambassador Mr. Withdraw to send a message to his office, and request him to strengthen surveillance around the embassy, for the time they remained inside.

He makes a call to Josué, informing him that they were at the Vilnius embassy. He asks him to inform his boss, Kenneth Díaz, that were safe with the other two men, but not to inform the ambassador, Mr Harrelson that his father was save at the Lithuanian embassy. Jack Brown's Strict Compliance Orders. Emphasizes that they have to keep it a secret that the mission is not over, until Mr. Harrelson was safe in America. It reminds him that in a few days, by reglamentary means, they will receive the official communication to the embassy.

Jack informs the ambassador, Mr. Glenn Withdraw, to keep in secret the release of the ambassador's father in Belarus, Mr. Harrelson and the other two persons. He had to keep the secret he housed them at the embassy, too. For all purposes, when they left the embassy, they had never been to it.

The ambassador understood and accepted what the GSSS agent asks him. They are agents attached directly to the government President office. Enything he asked for, or needed on a mission must provided immediately to him.

Later, along with the ambassador´s secretary, they gathered in the embassy dining room with the three liberated men. The relaxation was noticeable in the face of those present.

During lunch, Mr. Harrelson asked Jack if his son knew about his release.

- Due to, the circumstances we are now. -- Jack answers. -- We still have to keep track of his release. I have no doubt that they know our scape. I´m sure they´ll be looking for us all over the country. We will remain without contacting anyone, not even with your family, until each one is safe in London. It is my responsibility. Therefore, we will continue as before.

After lunch, the embassy provided them accommodation to rest. Jack advised them not to show outside for their safety. Every precaution was important. For the rest of the afternoon, Jack and the ambassador remained in lively conversation, waiting for the answer from agency.

Later, while waiting for news. Jack requested an office, to make a meticulous and detailed report of the mission carried out.

The report said:
"So as not to compromise our embassy, I took the decision to surround myself with personnel from outside the embassy. In support, I only asked Chief Kenneth Díaz to provide me with one of his men, Lt. Josué Kosher of Israeli origin. To whom I recommend for a promotion. He is enough prepared to carry out important missions, as well as, special services.

I detail also, the names with I formed the command, to be included in the Agency's report. I made special emphasis on the collaboration provided by Nikolay Ivanov, the brothers Alexander and Markus Krichenco and the mobster Fintan. They can considered as possible and necessary collaborators for future services. Logically, as long as they were well paid."

Once the report was finished, he used his secret key, to send it to Paul Blanchard.

Late at night, due to the changeof the time from one country to other. Jack receives the answer to his report. In it, he receives very specific orders regarding those released.

- Mister Brown. -- The ambassador asks him. -- Can I know what it says?

- Yes sir. Here you have the message.
"They will be provided with a new passport. We have reserved tickets for you at the KLM Co. bound for London tomorrow afternoon. So, have your passports issued. You must also provide them with a vehicle to take them to Riga's Lid Osta International Airport."

- There will be no problems. I will take in charge tomorrow the new passports be issued. -- The ambassador replies. -- And, I will arrange for you the transfer to the airport.

- Well, Sir. I think it is time for us to retire to rest. Tomorrow a hard day awaits us. Goodnight!

- Goodnight, Mr. Brown. See you tomorrow.

-oo0oo-

The day dawned cloudy. Although the weather forecast did not announce rain. It seemed that the Universal Flood was about to take place, from one moment to other. Fortunately, the meteorological part was right. The weather was cloudy but not rainy.

Moments later, all the guests gathered in the embassy dining room. They asked each other if they had any news of what the day had reserved for them.

The ambassador had instructed them to stay in the dining room, for being the best place, not to be seen. The ambassador put the chef of the embassy, to take care of serving the breakfast, and any drinks or food they asked for.

- Good morning, gentlemen. -- Who enters is Jack Brown. He gestures to the cook, to serve him breakfast. -- In a couple of hours, we will leave for the Riga airport. We are at a distance of about three hundred kilometers. It will take us about four hours to arrive.

We have reserved tickets for a flight to London. You can board without luggage. You´ll have new passports. The old ones, you will return them to me, before leaving, when I give you the new ones.

Although the eminent danger has passed, – He continued. – for security reason, we will not stop on the road. We need to have the maximum possible precaution, until we arrive at London. That is all for now. Thank you.

-ooOoo-

DESTINATION LONDON

They left the embassy in a minibus from the travel agency Riga Travel Tours. It was a non-stop trip along the way. The minibus was equipped with services. Jack wished to get to the airport as soon as possible.

It would take about four hours to get there. They had the plane tickets booked for the flight to London. Jack's priority was to get to the airport as soon as possible.

First, they would have to cross the Lithuania-Latvian border.

There were no problems with the new passports. It was only a matter of minutes. There was a special agreement, for diplomatic passport holders

Already at the airport, the driver took them directly to the VIP lounge of the passengers. Meanwhile they waited in the VIP lounge, Jack went KLM Air Co. reservation desk. He provided to the employee of the company the reservation key, to issued four tickets to London for the boarding card.

Back in the VIP lounge, he handed each passanger the boarding card, bound London.

Fifteen minutes later, a company stewardess picked up all the passengers, who waiting in the VIP Lounge, to accompany them the boarding gate.

They boarded first. Their preferent class tickets had priority. They looked at each other comforting themselves, when forty minutes later the aircraft took off, raising to the sky, in flight bound to London Heathrow International Airport.

Francois Renau and Richard Whitmore hugged each other and shook hands with a broad smile of relief and satisfaction on their faces. Now they were sure to feel free. They were flying back to their respective countries with their families.

-oo0oo-

CONFESSION TO MR. HARRELSON

Jack was traveling accompanied by Mr. Harrelson. Their seats were together. Mr. Harrelson took the opportunity to ask Jack, what had been the reason for his kidnapping.

- Mr. Brown. Could you tell me, if you know, the reasons why I was kidnapped? I never did anything illegal. I am a normal and honest person. Due to my age, I retired from my senatorial occupations for a few years. I consider that it was a mistake on the part of the Belarusian government to consider me a danger. Also, I do not understand how the government of my country has not tried to liberate me by official and diplomatic means. I've thought about that for a long time, what was the reason for my kidnapping.

- Mr Harrelson, I will tell you the reasons why you were kidnapped. But you have to promise me that you will keep the secret, until your son be officially informed.

- Yes sir, I promise you. But what does my son have to do with this?

"Fortunately, neither of you have committed any illegal act, but they used you to leak "classified and top secret documents". They took out secret informaction threatening your son to kill you. They needed to hold you, to blackmail your son. -- During the flight, Jack detailed him the reason for his kidnapping. -- As you will understand now, holding you in prision was the reason for blackmailing him leaking high-level information.

Mr. Francois Renau is a Belgian Diplomat. They kidnapped to exchange him for a KGB agent, who is a prisoner in Belgium.

Regarding to Agent Richard Whitmore, he had assigned as Commercial Attaché to his embassy. They arrested him by spy. They would use him to get the most information or to be used also as a money currency."

When Mr. Harrelson really knew the reasons for his kidnapping, he could not contain any longer and began to cry silently.

- Thank you very much, Mr. Brown or whatever your name is. -- He says. Holding his hand, in a loving and sincere gesture of gratitude. -- If you had not taken me out of that prison, what woul have happened to me?

- Do you honestly want me to answer you, Mr. Harrelson? -- Jack nodded to him. -- Do you really want to know?

- Yes. I would appreciate it!

- The truth is that, you have been very lucky. I don't think you would have lasted long. You practically had your days counted. Your son worked with them, passing classified documents to keep you alive. What your son does not know is that the documents that lately received were not importants. The leak of documents was known in our country. So they sent me to find out the person who was delivering them information.

- And now, what will happen to my son?

- Possibly, he will return to our country. I really don't know what he's going to face. They will removed from his office or put on trial. You must calm down. You will serve as a mitigating factor and as attenuating for your kidnapping. He hasn´t given any information for money. I want your word to stand firm, until everything is settled.

- You have my word and my thanks. -- He wiped away his tears and they both leaned back in their seats. They would rest a few hours before arriving at London Heathrow Airport.

The flight from the KLM Company landed at Heathrow Airport at nineteen hours.

Police and customs control passed quickly. They had no luggage. The farewell was most emotional, especially by Mr. Francois Renau.

Mister Renau, unfortunately, the man did not even have to make a phone call. Jack gave him five hundred pounds to pay for his ticket to Brussels, and have enough money left for his expenses, and to pay for a hotel night.

Agent Whitmore made a call to his office. Later, he identified to a police patrol on duty at the airport. They immediately took him in the direction of Scotland Yard Headquarters.

When agent Whitmore said goodbye, he reminded Jack that he would always be at his disposal, selflessly and whenever he needed it. They said goodbye with a hug and a handshake.

Jack Brown and Mr. Harrelson spent that night staying at one of the Heathrow airport hotels. They had booked two tickets with the company American Airlines, for the next day to Washington DC. That afternoon, there was no possibility of departure. The flights were full booked. The departure will be for the next morning.

-ooOoo-

HOMECOMING

It was twelve oclock at London. The American Airlines flight was taking off from London Heathrow International Airport to Washington, D.C.

At fourteen hours, Washington, DC. Local time the aircraft of the American Airlines landed at Washington-Dulles.

Paul Blanchard was waiting for him at the exit of the police and customs control. Theodore (Jack Brown) had an unexpected and pleasant surprise. Along with his boss and friend was his wife Claudia waiting for him. Without thinking about it, they ran to meet each other, melting into a tight hug.

- Thanks Paul. You don't know how much I appreciate the detail.

- Thanks to you for coming back. You don't know how many times, Claudia has called me asking for news of you. -- Paul comments. -- I thought it was only my wife, who behaved like her.

- Paul, allow me to introduce you to Mr. Harrelson Senior, father of our ambassador to Belarus.

- A great pleasure, Mr. Harrelson. You do not know how happy it is to have you among with us again, in these difficult moments. -- He greets him, holding out his hand. -- Please, let's go out, I have a vehicle outside. The big boss is waiting for us in his office.

The vehicle was a black limousine. Theodore and Claudia sat together. They had many things to talk about, although they remained silent. It was not the right time nor the place.

When they arrived at the agency's offices, A.S. Import & Export International, Miss Margaret, Nicholas Smith´s secretary, received them.

She immediately put them in the chief's office, Nicholas Smith. Meanwhile, Claudia waited in the company of Miss Margaret, who tried to make her waiting as pleasant as possible, showing her from one of the office windows, the views of the great avenues with the most interesting monuments of the city.

An hour later, after the meeting, Nicholas Smith accompanied their visitors to the exit. He took the opportunity to greet Claudia.

- Mrs. Georges, I am delighted to meet you. May I call you Claudia?

- Of course, I have no problem, Mr. Smith, sorry Nicholas.

Everyone grasped the meaning of the answer, especially Mr. Smith, who kissed Claudia, while smiling on both cheeks.

- Well Theodore, we will take care of the rest. Claudia, I sincerely regret having deprived of your husband's company all this time. But the truth was that he was the only one to carry out this work, as fortunately it has been. In compensation, you have reserved a suite at the Park Plaza Hotel, as long as you want. I have no doubt that you will enjoy it.

- Chief, I have no more clothes what I am wearing. In this way they will not allow me to enter in the hotel.

- Well, use the card but without going over, the agency has many extra expenses lately.

- Okay chief. Goodbye everybody. He caught Claudia by the waist and they quickly left the office.

Before reaching the hotel, they came in one of the best men's shops in the city. Theodore, bought two suits with its accessories; shirts, ties, and underwear.

In the Joe's Deluxe Shoes, he bought two pairs of shoes to match the suits. They stopped a taxi to take them to the hotel. The suite was spectacular; it was located on the top floor of the hotel with magnificent views.

While Theodore put the clothes in the closet, Claudia prepared the bathroom. A short time later, he heard Claudia voice. She was claiming him.

- Theo the bath is ready. Don't be late.

When Theo entered the bathroom, she was sitting in the bath, ready to share it.

-oo0oo-

They spent a wonderful week in Washington DC. Claudia did not ask about the mission in Belarus. Now what did mattered to her was that he had returned, and was with her. From what Paul Blanchard had said, the mission had been a great success.

At the agency, he was highly regarded. Days later, he received recognition from the President.

Claudia was immensely happy to have him back home with her. She hoped they would never separate him from her again.

That was what really her wish. That they never would call him
again. Ever again.

But................

-oo0oo-

MCG.
1

www.ingramcontent.com/pod-product-compliance
Lightning Source LLC
Chambersburg PA
CBHW020331160726
47992CB00004B/1803